P9-EDG-912

Flair's eyes blazed with sudden fury

"Just because you pay me a salary doesn't mean you've bought me body and soul—that clause wasn't in the contract," Flair exclaimed.

The startling blue of Luke's eyes darkened at that, and he took a step toward her. Alarmed, Flair moved quickly but he moved faster. He caught her wrist and held it as he drew her closer, his eyes like ice in his sunburned face. Flair opened her mouth to protest, but before she could his lips were on hers, keeping them apart.

"Do you think I've bought you body and soul now?" he asked huskily. "Maybe I don't need to buy...maybe you'd rather give? But I won't ask you yet, Flair. Not until you're ready...."

NICOLA WEST
is also the author of this
Harlequin Romance

2526—DEVIL'S GOLD

This title may be available at your local bookseller.

For a free catalog listing all titles currently available,
send your name and address to:

HARLEQUIN READER SERVICE
1440 South Priest Drive, Tempe, AZ 85281
Canadian address: Stratford, Ontario N5A 6W2

NICOLA WEST

lucifer's brand

Harlequin Books

TORONTO • NEW YORK • LOS ANGELES • LONDON
AMSTERDAM • PARIS • SYDNEY • HAMBURG
STOCKHOLM • ATHENS • TOKYO • MILAN

Harlequin Presents first edition April 1983
ISBN 0-373-10589-4

Original hardcover edition published in 1982
by Mills & Boon Limited

Copyright © 1982 by Nicola West. All rights reserved.
Philippine copyright 1982. Australian copyright 1982.
Cover illustration copyright © 1983 by Tom Bjarnason Inc.
Except for use in any review, the reproduction or utilization of
this work in whole or in part in any form by any electronic,
mechanical or other means, now known or hereafter invented,
including xerography, photocopying and recording, or in any
information storage or retrieval system, is forbidden without
the permission of the publisher, Harlequin Enterprises Limited,
225 Duncan Mill Road, Don Mills, Ontario, Canada M3B 3K9.

All the characters in this book have no existence outside the
imagination of the author and have no relation whatsoever to
anyone bearing the same name or names. They are not even
distantly inspired by any individual known or unknown to the
author, and all the incidents are pure invention.

The Harlequin trademarks, consisting of the words
HARLEQUIN PRESENTS and the portrayal of a Harlequin,
are trademarks of Harlequin Enterprises Limited and are
registered in the Canada Trade Marks Office; the portrayal
of a Harlequin is registered in the United States Patent
and Trademark Office.

Printed in U.S.A.

CHAPTER ONE

'THE City of Lights!'

Flair Pattison gazed down at the panorama of colours spread in the velvety blackness below, and the woman beside her smiled with amusement.

'You can see now why the Apollo astronauts called it that,' she remarked. 'Perth was one of the places they flew over at night, and it really impressed them. Of course, it's beautiful by day as well.'

'I'm sure it is.' Flair stared eagerly from the window of the jumbo jet as it circled the city, preparing to land. 'My father's told me a lot about it in his letters.'

'You're going to have some reunion,' Jean Chapman observed, watching the excited green eyes under the cap of smooth auburn hair. 'How long is it since you've seen each other?'

'Nine years,' Flair confessed. 'Dad came out to Australia when I was thirteen. There wasn't any real quarrel—he and Mum had been more or less separated for some time, though we all still lived together. Then when he got the chance of a partnership out here with an old friend, he decided to take it. He was so sick of the way architecture was going in England—planning restrictions and spec building—he jumped at the chance. And as Mum wasn't prepared to leave her own career, she and I stayed behind. It was all quite amicable.'

'But you must have missed him,' the older woman guessed.

'Oh, yes. Yes, I did.' Flair turned away to gaze out of the window again. Even now, with the pain of separation soon to be assuaged, she could still find it difficult to speak of those empty years after her father had gone. Oh, he had written often, phoned on her birthday and at Christmas, kept as close a contact as was possible—but there had still been times when she lay wide-eyed and miserable at night, wondering how he was and what he was doing. Wondering if she would ever see him again.

And at last here she was. Within the next hour they would be together again. She turned impulsively to Jean and was momentarily surprised by a look of equal excitement on the older woman's features as she too gazed down at the brilliantly-lit city below. Flair bit her lip and rebuked herself for her selfishness. As if she were the only person on the plane to be excited! She watched Jean's brown eyes glow, saw her hand shake slightly as she raised it to flick a strand of dark hair away from her cheek, and her voice softened as she asked:

'Are your family meeting you at the airport? You must be longing to see them again.'

Jean flashed her a quick look of appreciation and answered, 'Yes, Robert will be there—that's my husband—and Carl, our elder boy. The other one's away at uni—university—in Melbourne. He graduated from Perth and he's doing an extra course there.'

'You must be proud of him—of both of them.'

'Mm, too right! It was a shame neither of them

could go back to England with me—Mum and Dad would have loved to see them, they were just babies when we emigrated. Of course, what we'd really like is for Mum and Dad to come out to us—permanently—and maybe they will when Dad retires, which won't be long now.'

'It can't be easy when your children go off to the other side of the world,' Flair said thoughtfully. Rather to her surprise, she had found herself missing her own mother already, and wondering if Susan was missing her. There had been no lack of encouragement for Flair to make the trip—Susan had never been a clinging mother—but what had her innermost thoughts really been? Had she wondered, as she waved Flair off at Heathrow only yesterday, whether she would ever see her daughter again? Had she gone away to shed tears Flair had never seen?

Shaken by these thoughts, Flair had been grateful for Jean's company on the flight. The older woman had seemed to sense the unexpected fears Flair had been experiencing; her comforting presence and casual conversation had done a lot to calm them. Flair hoped very much that she would be able to meet Jean again, in Perth. She had a feeling that when you came to a new country you could do with all the friends you could get.

'Did you say you were going to stay here for a while, get a job?' Jean's voice broke in on her thoughts. Flair wrenched her mind back to the present and nodded.

'Yes, that's right. Personal assistant to a hotelier Dad's doing some work for. I've trained in catering and hotel management, you see—got all the certificates and worked in several English hotels, and I thought it would be a good idea to get some experience in Australia.'

'Sounds a great idea. Have you worked in any of the real big hotels? The London ones?'

Flair smiled. 'Oh yes. I did a year at Claridge's. It was hard work, though—the glamour doesn't seep behind the scenes! I've had quite wide experience, really—started at a country hotel in the Cotswolds, then moved on to Manchester, then I did a stint as a relief, working at different places all over the country for just two or three weeks at a time while the managers were on holiday—that sort of thing.' She smiled, remembering the toil, the crises and the fun of that period. 'Then I went to London. That was interesting, and I got a lot of experience there, but I wouldn't like to work there always. I like to be able to get into the country a bit more.'

'Well, I think you'll enjoy working in Perth,' Jean commented. 'It's a capital city, but it's compact and there's plenty of outdoor life, what with the beaches for swimming and surfing, and all the sport you could want. D'you know which hotel you'll be working in?'

'The Seager Hotel,' Flair said, and the other woman's eyes widened.

'Seager's? You mean you'll be working for Luke Seager? Oh-oh-you're in for an exciting time, then!'

'An exciting time?' A small frown appeared on Flair's elfin features. 'What do you mean?'

'Why, haven't you heard of Luke Seager? No, I suppose you won't have. He's pretty well known in Australia, I can tell you. Owns a chain of hotels—

built them up almost from nothing after his father died—a real go-getter. And that goes for women too—they say no one's ever resisted him. Wish I had the chance to try, that's all! Only don't tell Robert I said so!' She looked at Flair, taking in the heart-shaped face, the slender yet provocative figure so beautifully emphasised by a cool, loosely-cut pant suit in cream linen. An emerald scarf at the neck reflected the colour of Flair's eyes and set off her bronze hair. 'Like I said, you're in for an exciting time.'

'I doubt it,' Flair said stiffly. 'A man like that will have his pick of women. He won't want an affair with his personal assistant. And even if he did——' she shrugged '—I'm pretty well able to take care of myself.'

'Well, you just watch out if that's the way you feel,' Jean advised. 'Luke Seager's got a real reputation. They say he's the most dangerous man in Western Australia, as far as women are concerned. Not that I've ever heard anyone complaining.' She smiled suddenly. 'Know what they call him? Lucifer! They say once he's kissed you, you're branded for life. You'll never be free of him again. So if you don't want that kind of excitement, maybe you'd better go work in a department store. I don't give much for your chances as P.A. to Luke Seager!'

Flair stared at her, conscious of a strange thrill somewhere deep in her stomach. It could have been fear—or it could have been something else. Impatiently, she bent to gather up her flight bag. Luke Seager was to be her employer, nothing more. Why, surely her father would never have arranged

the job for her if he'd thought Luke the kind of man
to take advantage of her position. And if he did turn
out to be the sort who couldn't keep his hands off
anything in skirts—well, there were other jobs, no
doubt. Irresistible, indeed! He'd soon find out she
was no easy game, she reflected as the plane bumped
down and taxied across the tarmac. Flair Pattison
hadn't come all this way to succumb to the first con-
ceited male she came into contact with—no way!
She had her sights set too firmly on her career.

After filling in immigration forms and a cursory
Customs check, Flair was at last free to go through
the barrier towards the excited crowd of Australians,
most of them dressed casually in open-necked shirts,
light dresses and even tracksuits, waiting to greet
friends and relatives. She paused, eyeing them doubt-
fully, wondering where her father was, if he had even
arrived. She had his address, of course, and presumably there would be taxis to take if he didn't turn
up—but just as her thoughts pursued this rather bleak
path, a sudden movement on the edge of the crowd
caught her eye, and she turned to see Jeff Pattison
striding towards her, his arms held out in welcome.

Flair stood quite still, almost unable for a moment
to cope with the emotions that shook her body. She
watched as her father strode towards her, seeing him
for the first time for nine years as a flesh and blood
man rather than an image in a photograph; seeing
his coppery hair, so like her own even though it was
now faded by sun and the years, the green eyes that
she had inherited. The tall, lean body moved loosely
and easily, and as he came nearer Flair saw his teeth
flash in a grin of pure delight. In that moment, she

knew that she had not come merely to a strange country; she had come home.

'Dad! Dad, how marvellous!' Any more words were lost in the bear-hug he gave her, and she clung to him, her eyes wet with emotion at meeting the father she hadn't seen for nine years. 'Dad, how are you?'

'I'm good.' He held her away from him, scanning her face. 'My word, you've grown up a real beauty, Flair. A touch of our Australian sun and you'll knock 'em all for six!'

Flair chuckled. 'You know you've gone all Australian, Dad? I never really noticed it on the phone. But how are you really—you're looking a bit tired.'

'Well, what do you expect when I have to stay up half the night to meet planes?' he countered, smiling. 'Is this all your luggage? Good job you managed to get a trolley. Look, will you wait by the entrance here while I go and get the car? It's a Holden estate, yellow. I won't be more'n a few minutes.' He paused and touched her cheek gently. 'It's great to have you out here, Flair,' he said quietly. 'What I've always dreamed of. We'll have a great time together.' And with a quick smile he strode off into the darkness.

Flair stood waiting with her luggage, lifting her face to the soft night air. It had a cool freshness welcome after the warmth of the plane, though she guessed the temperature to be around seventy, heavenly to anyone from England but no more than spring to Australians. A tiny frown puckered her brow. She hadn't missed the way Jeff had evaded

her question about how he was. And he did look
tired—more tired than a late night should account
for. Older, too—though she supposed that was in-
evitable, considering the time they had been apart.
Maybe he was working too hard. This Luke Seager,
that he had the big contract with—maybe he was a
slave-driver as well as a rake. Well, she'd soon alter
that. Dad hadn't had anyone to look after him all
these years, but that had changed now, and Luke
Seager would soon see that he had someone to reckon
with in his new personal assistant. She would be in a
position to see exactly what went on, and if she didn't
like it the sparks would fly.

Flair had no false modesty about her own abilities.
Brought up by a career-minded mother whose marriage had proved to be a mistake, she had decided
long ago that her own career would take priority
over that of any man. And if that meant staying
single, so be it. She had no knowledge of passion;
her mother had always dismissed love as being vastly
overrated and marriage mostly for the benefit of
men, who took a promising woman with plenty of
potential and turned her into a cabbage and household drudge. Without ever bearing any malice towards Jeff, Susan had nevertheless managed to make
it clear that marriage was a mistake she wouldn't
make again; and Flair, without consciously realising
it, had imbibed her ideas and coloured them with
her own.

On leaving school, she had trained enthusiastically
in all aspects of the hotel trade. Experience in several
of the best hotels, in both the country and London,
had taken her to the position of being able to pick

and choose her next job; when Jeff had written suggesting a long visit to Australia, it had seemed an ideal opportunity to widen her knowledge, taking her a step further along the path to her ultimate ambition which was to manage a large hotel entirely on her own.

The arrival of the yellow Holden brought her back to the present, and between them she and Jeff soon had her cases packed into the capacious estate car. She settled herself beside her father, and they drove off towards the suburb where he lived.

'You're going to love it here,' Jeff said easily as they passed through the quiet streets. 'Especially now, with spring in full swing. There's nothing like the Western Australian wildflowers, you know. Thousands of them, all different, and all colours of the rainbow. Makes the bush look like one huge opal.'

'I've been looking forward to it,' Flair assented. 'I'm hoping we'll have time to go around a bit together before I start work—or will you be too busy?'

'Too busy? With my only daughter in Australia for the first time?' Jeff laughed. 'No, Luke knows the score, and his is the biggest contract I've got just now. I daresay we'll be able to manage something.'

Luke. The name brought again that odd twist to the stomach that Flair had experienced earlier. Trying to appear casual, she said, 'Tell me about Mr Seager, Dad. Since he's going to be my employer, I'd like to know a bit about him.'

'Well, for a start you won't be calling him Mr Seager—we go in for first names here. I don't know that there's much to tell about him really. Practically a self-made man—inherited a pretty rocky business, just a couple of run-down hotels, when his father died, built them up and now he's got a fast-expanding chain. The job I'm on is the design for a new leisure complex on a small island a bit north of here. Should be very nice—Spanish-style buildings, separate chalets for those who want a bit of privacy, swimming-pools, squash courts—just about whatever you want. Actually, it's almost finished—we're starting to think about the next now, a motel down the coast near Albany. Yes, Luke Seager's certainly coming big.' He swung the big car into a pleasant street lined with exotic trees and shrubs. 'Well, here we are—Yokine. This is home. Nice to have you here, Flair.'

Flair got out of the car, suddenly conscious of an immense weariness. The flight had lasted for over twenty hours, with only one stop for fuel at Bombay; the emotion of meeting her father again after so long seemed to have drained her of any further energy. She stood on the grass at the side of the road, swaying a little, and her father slipped his arm round her shoulders.

'You're all in, Flair,' he said kindly. 'Why don't you just bring in what you need for now and go straight to bed? I'll make a cup of tea, and then I'll fetch in the rest of the luggage.'

The sun was streaming into Flair's bedroom when she woke next morning and she rolled over, realising with delight where she was. The trip had been planned and dreamed of for so long that it seemed almost unbelievable that she was actually here; but as she lay there a shout of raucous, chuckling laughter from somewhere outside first startled her, then brought a broad smile to her face as she realised she was hearing her first kookaburra.

The bungalow was quiet. Jeff had told her last night that he would probably be going in to his office first thing and would see her at lunchtime, giving her the morning in which to potter quietly about and recover from the long journey. She gazed around the room, enjoying its light airiness and the coolness of its green and white colour scheme. Jeff had designed and built this bungalow several years ago, she remembered, and felt sad that he had never had anyone to share it with him. But perhaps he was like his wife Susan and felt that marriage was a mistake to make only once. Certainly they both seemed happy enough on their own, Susan with the girls' boarding school of which she was headmistress in Surrey, Jeff with his architectural practice here.

And so would she be, Flair determined as the thought of Luke Seager crept unbidden into her mind. She had never yet met the man who could take and possess her heart—or, indeed, any other part of her. And she didn't expect to now—whatever the female population of Australia might think! Anyway, she had met plenty of men in England who fancied themselves as rakes and irresistible to women. She had managed to resist them without any trouble, and she didn't suppose that Luke Seager, who by all accounts had never been out of Australia, was going to be any more of a threat. Why, he was probably downright uncouth in comparison with the sophisticated and urbane men she was accustomed to in London. No, she had no doubt at all as to her abilities to handle the man they called Lucifer.

Aware of hunger, she slid out of bed and padded across to the adjoining bathroom. A quick shower freshened her, and she dressed in cool slacks and shirt in matching avocado green before making her way to the kitchen; then, armed with a tall glass of orange juice and a dish of bran flakes, she wandered out through the mesh fly-screen door to the patio and sank down on a long sun-lounger beside the small swimming-pool.

At first, the light dazzled her; it seemed so much clearer and brighter than at home, and the sky was a deeper, more intense blue than she had ever seen in England.

The sun was pleasantly warm, though she supposed that as it was still only early October, the temperature would rise a good deal higher in another month or so; her father had told her last night that there was still rain about and the weather could be unpredictable for another three or four weeks. To the Australians themselves, today might still be on the chilly side; to Flair it was heavenly and she stretched out comfortably, promising herself to do some sunbathing later, perhaps even to have a swim.

The garden was full of flowers and outside the fence she could see the tall eucalyptus trees that grew in front of the house. As she lay there she heard the melodic warbling of a black and white bird very similar to an English magpie but without the long tail; a brightly-coloured parrot brought a gasp of surprise from her throat when it perched on an overhead wire, and from somewhere nearby she heard again the unmistakable chortle of the kooka-burra.

For a while, Flair dozed pleasantly in the sunshine. Then, thinking that she might as well be improving her suntan, she went indoors and changed into a brief bikini of dazzling white with a gold motif round the edges. And when she came out again, revelling in the feel of warm sunshine on her bare skin, it seemed a crime not to dive straight into the swimming-pool.

She had completed several lengths, both above and under water, when she heard a cheerful whistle from the house and turned on her back to see who was coming.

'Out here, Dad,' she called. 'I couldn't resist it— the sun was so lovely. Do you manage to swim all the year ro—oh!'

Her voice trailed away as she saw that the new-comer wasn't her father after all, but a complete stranger. A man of about thirty-five, tall, broad and blond, dressed casually but devastatingly in pale blue slacks and navy shirt unbuttoned almost to the waist. Casually, with the easy grace of a tiger, he lounged into view and a look of sudden interest replaced the curiosity on his face as he took in her appearance as she floated, slender and almost naked, in the blue water.

Flair stared at him, feeling flustered and confused. Who was he, to come marching into her father's garden without so much as a by-your-leave? She shook the wet hair from her eyes and said angrily: 'My father's out. Perhaps you'd like to leave a message. I expect you know where the door is, since you came in by it.'

His eyes widened and Flair felt a distinct shock, as if she'd received a sudden blow to the chest. She didn't think she'd ever seen eyes of such a deep blue before; it was almost sapphire, and all the more startling next to the deeply-tanned golden brown skin of the man's face and the burnished corn-gold of his hair. He looked at her for a moment and then said easily: 'No, I don't think I'll leave a message. I'd rather stick around till he comes. Anyway, he won't be long.'

'How—how do you know that?' Flair gasped, standing upright and checking hastily to see that the bra of her bikini was in place; the man's eyes seemed to be everywhere, and were registering a good deal of interest in her almost naked curves.

'Because he sent me round here ahead of him. Said he was sure we'd like to meet as soon as possible, get to know each other a bit.' The amusement in the level tones flicked at her nerves and she retorted furiously: 'I don't believe you! Look, if you're some kind of salesman, you'd better go. I've told you, I'll give my father any message you like to leave. There's no need for you to waste your time.'

'Oh, I'm not wasting my time.' The long body coiled down on the edge of the pool close beside her and Flair's eyes were drawn reluctantly to the strength and power implicit in the well-muscled thighs revealed as his pale blue slacks tightened round them. She raised her eyes, noting unwillingly the broad shoulders that tapered to a slim waist, speaking of a superbly-fit body that seemed to exude an almost tangible male virility; then her eyes caught again that startling blue glance and she looked away, blushing furiously.

'No, I wouldn't say I was wasting my time,' he went on musingly, his eyes frankly assessing her own body in the now embarrassingly brief bikini. 'In fact, I can't really think of a nicer way to spend a sunny spring morning. . . . You're not getting cold in there, are you?'

'No!' she denied at once, trying not to shiver, but now that she had stopped swimming she was beginning to feel distinctly chilled. And what's more, she thought ruefully, he knew it, damn him! If only he'd *go*.

'Well, if I were you I'd warm up with a couple more lengths and then hop out,' he advised. 'It's still a mite early for swimming—although I suppose you're used to the cold, coming from England.'

'How do you know——' she began, then stopped herself. What was she doing, getting into any kind of conversation with this—this intruder? 'Look,' she said coldly, 'I've asked you several times now to go. If you like to leave your name and address and tell me whatever business you're in, I'll see that my father has your message as soon as he comes home. Now, if you don't mind, I want to get out and do a little sunbathing—alone. I had a long journey yesterday and I'm rather tired.'

'Is that so?' He made no attempt to move and the amusement in his eyes was quite unmistakable now. Flair bit her lip with annoyance and frustration, then drew back in the water as he suddenly held out a hand to her.

'Come on, Miss Pattison,' he encouraged her. 'Why don't you just hop out and do your sunbathing with me? I'm not such an ogre as all that, you know—I won't eat you. Not today, anyway,' he added half to himself as his eyes once more slid over her body in appreciation of its curved slenderness.

'I've *told* you——' she began furiously, then gasped as a powerful hand gripped her by the wrist and jerked her bodily from the pool, another hand coming round to support her body on its way out. For a moment, Flair was conscious of a hard body close to her own; a wave of heat, of maleness that seemed to emanate from every pore, so that she felt momentarily dizzy with the sheer vitality that assailed her senses. Strong limbs encircled her as she struggled; then she was dumped on the side of the pool and as she shook the dripping hair from her eyes she realised he was laughing at her.

'How *dare* you!' she expostulated, scrambling to her feet, all too aware of the unsophisticated picture she must present. 'How dare you come here, un-invited, take possession of my father's garden, order me about, *drag* me—Just who are you anyway?' she demanded, tilting her chin to look up at him, think-ing even in the midst of her anger that he must be a good six feet tall. 'Because whoever you are, for whatever reason you came here today I shall take very good care to see that you don't come again! When my father hears about the way you've behaved, he'll—well, he'll make sure that whatever your business is with him he'll find someone else. And he's not without influence around here, you know—you may find yourself losing a lot of business through your behaviour this morning!'

The blue eyes met hers, still glinting with amusement. 'Just what kind of business do you imagine I'm in?' he enquired silkily.

Flair shrugged. 'I don't know, do I?' she pointed out. 'Since you've consistently refused to tell me. But from your persistence and your smoothness, I should say you were in some kind of insurance.'

At that, he burst out laughing, while Flair, almost at the edge of her patience, picked up her towel from the sunlounger and wrapped it around herself, feeling more confident now that she was covered. 'Well, are you?' she demanded at last.

The blond giant stopped laughing and looked down at her. His mouth was still twitching and Flair thought how she would love to hit it really hard, wipe that laughter from his eyes and lips, show that she was something rather more than the amusing child he seemed to think her. Then he reached out and laid a hand on each shoulder, and at his touch Flair's skin tingled and she seemed to feel each finger separately, even through the thick folds of the towel, so that she moved aside impatiently.

'No, Miss Pattison,' he said at length, his voice sober now though Flair could still detect the amusement in it. 'No, I'm not an insurance salesman. And I doubt very much if your father will run me out of town when he finds me here—especially as he really did tell me to come along, you know. You may have heard of me—indeed, I hope you have, since I guess we're going to be seeing quite a lot of each other in the future. I'm Luke Seager—the man you're father's doing a fair bit of work for just at present. The man you're going to work for as personal assistant.'

Flair drew the towel closer around her, aware of a sudden chill. Luke Seager! The man they called Lucifer. Whose kiss was said to be irresistible. Who was to be her employer, as at present he was her father's, and who was even now keeping that bright, direct gaze on her face, watching her, assessing her every reaction.

Oh God! Did things *have* to go wrong the moment she set foot in Australia?

'Maybe we should start again,' he offered, smiling, and his teeth flashed dazzlingly against the golden tan. 'May I introduce myself? Luke Seager, at your service.' He swept her an exaggerated bow. 'That's the way they do things in England, isn't it?'

Flair felt herself flush with annoyance. He was *still* laughing at her. And she couldn't take the hand he was holding out without letting the towel go, and it wasn't at all securely fastened around her. The fact that Luke Seager had already seen exactly what she looked like underneath didn't seem to make any difference. She didn't want that piercing glance roaming over her body again.

'You don't want to shake hands?' he pursued, moving a little closer so that she was aware once more of that aura of masculinity that surrounded him. 'Of course, in France they kiss, don't they? Even the men. Like this——' Before she could stop him, he had a hand on each arm and had kissed her quickly on each cheek, leaving two bright spots of fire where his lips had been. 'Or like this . . .' And his arms slid round her, drawing her close as his mouth fastened on hers, opening it with an expertise that was both gentle and inexorable. The sheer un-

expectedness of it left Flair helpless for a moment.
Fire and weakness together ran down her body, setting her heart to a wild beating that had the blood
racing through her veins. Her legs seemed to lose all
strength and she felt that she would have collapsed
had it not been for Luke's arms holding her strongly
against him. She felt his body move against hers and
a stifled gasp escaped her as she became aware of
the hardness of his limbs, telling her all too clearly of
his desire. With a sudden panic-stricken conviction
that another second would be too late, she tried to
wrench herself free. But the arms that held her were
ready for her struggles. They tightened their grip,
holding her ever closer, the hands moving, sliding
the towel up her body until it could be pulled away
entirely. She felt Luke Seager move a fraction away
from her as the towel was pulled away from between
them and thrown to the ground; then she was jerked
back against him, gasping as she felt his hands move
possessively over the bare skin of her back, sliding
down until the fingers were touching the top of her
bikini   briefs,   inserting   themselves   under   the
band. . . .

The world seemed to spin round her as Flair
moaned under his touch. Feeling that she must fall,
she let her own hands, trapped between their bodies,
spread out against his chest, feeling the hair and skin
under his thin shirt. Dazed, almost unaware of what
she did, she let her fingers slip into the warmth
within. Luke Seager . . . Lucifer . . . Jean Chapman's
words came back into her mind, as vividly as if she
had just heard them spoken, and the full realisation
of what was happening flooded over her. Horrified,

she twisted suddenly in his arms and broke away, stumbling over the towel as she backed out of his reach and stared at him with wide, appalled eyes.

'Well,' he drawled at last, and she realised that they were both breathing quickly. 'You're quite a bombshell, Miss Pattison, you know that? Or—now that we've introduced ourselves—maybe I can call you Flair? Who gave you that name, by the way? Was it because of your red hair?'

'It's auburn,' she snapped, snatching up the towel again. 'And it's not spelt the way you seem to think—it's a-i-r, not a-r-e. Look, if you don't mind, Mr Seager, I think I'll go in and get dressed. My father shouldn't be long now and——'

'But surely,' he interrupted, 'you came out here to sunbake. Don't let me stop you. And drop the Mr Seager, won't you? I'm Luke. We don't go a lot for formality around here.'

Flair hesitated. She was reluctant to go in and dress, feeling that if she did that Luke Seager would in some indefinable way have scored a point. Yet she was equally unwilling to abandon the towel again and stretch on the lounger under his bright, appraising gaze—especially after what had just happened. She felt her face burn again at the memory of that kiss and—worse still—her own reaction to it. She would never have believed that she could respond in such a way to a man she had met only minutes before—to any man, come to that. Nobody had ever kissed Flair that way before—with her mother's example in front of her, together with her sheltered upbringing at the boarding school and her own firm ambitions, she'd made sure that no man had ever got within kissing distance, though there had been the succession of casual dates for parties, dances and so on, none of which had meant anything more than a pleasant evening out. So the sensations that had surged through her body when Luke Seager held her in his arms and probed her mouth with his, the fire that had raced through her veins and the delicious swimming of her brain, were all unfamiliar to her. Unfamiliar, disturbing—and frightening. And she determined that she would never let herself be exposed to them again.

'Come on,' he murmured, his voice like silk. 'Why don't you relax, Flair? Stretch out on that lounger and tell me all about yourself. I've known Jeff Pattison a good many years now. I've been looking forward to meeting his daughter.'

'You won't be so pleased with yourself when I tell him how you've been behaving this morning,' she retorted. 'And if you think *he'll* be pleased——' She stopped as Luke took a step forward and gripped her arms, holding her so tightly that tears of pain sprang to her eyes.

'But you won't be telling him, will you?' he ground out. 'You won't be telling him, Flair honey—and shall I tell you why? Mainly because you asked for everything you got and more, however much you may pretend to be the demure little English rosebud. And also because your father doesn't employ *me—I* employ *him*. And my contract's worth a good deal to him. He won't thank you for breaking that up. You'd better believe it!'

He released her as suddenly as he had grasped her, and Flair stared up at him, her eyes wide with shock as she slowly rubbed her bruised arms. She wanted to repudiate what he had just said; wanted to shout at him that it didn't matter, he could take his contracts elsewhere, they would manage without him—but she knew she couldn't do that. Jeff was relying heavily on this work with Seager Hotels, he'd hinted as much last night. He couldn't afford to lose it. And it wouldn't be a good start to her visit to Australia to destroy his livelihood on the first morning she arrived.

'Seeing sense?' Luke Seager asked softly.

Suddenly blinded by tears, Flair turned abruptly away. 'All right, you win,' she said shakily. 'I won't say anything. But don't ever touch me again, that's all. I don't like it, do you hear? *I don't like it!*'

Luke Seager laughed softly. 'You really sound as if you mean that——'

'I do!' she interrupted hotly.

'—but you can't fool me,' he went on as if she hadn't spoken. 'Don't like it, eh! Flair Pattison, you're one of the hottest little properties I've ever had the good fortune to lay my hands on. Why, do you know I can't believe my luck that you're going to be my personal assistant! We're going to have a great time together, you and I.' He held out his hand and let a finger trail slowly down the soft skin of her inner arm. 'Come on, Flair honey,' he went on coaxingly, 'forget this pretence of not liking it and let's start getting to know each other.'

Flair felt every inch of her body freeze. She was burningly aware of the trail his finger had just drawn down her arm. His dark eyes bored into hers and she felt her heart thundering in her breast.

Taking a deep breath, she slowly wrapped the towel around her trembling body. Her mother's success as a headmistress after her dismissal of love and marriage came back to her, strengthening her own resolve. She remembered her determination to get to the top in her own chosen career; remembered the hard work of her training, the struggle to be recognised in a world still largely dominated by men. A moment's madness—a moment's unexpected sensuality—these couldn't be allowed to ruin all she'd worked for. And now that she was aware of this unsuspected streak in her own nature, she would be better able to guard against it. Luke Seager was going to discover that there was one girl in the world who didn't find him irresistible. Maybe the discovery would even do him good!

'I'm sorry, Mr Seager,' she said coldly. 'You seem to have got the wrong idea about me. I'm really *not* interested in an affair, with you or anyone else. I came out here to see my father and to work. The job you offered seemed ideal, but if there are strings attached it would be better for us both if we get it clear now that I'm not looking for that kind of work. If that's all you have to offer, I'll look somewhere else.' She drew the towel closer around her, unaware of the seductiveness it lent her figure. 'I hope I haven't wasted your time, Mr Seager. I'm sure you'll soon find some other girl who'll be . . . willing. And now, I'm going to get dressed. Dad should be here any time now.'

She turned to go, but felt herself grasped for the third time by Luke Seager's iron hand. This time, she kept control of herself, though intensely aware of his fingers encircling her arm. She stood quite still, not looking at him.

'So you've had your say,' he grated, and she heard with a tremor of fear the anger in his voice. 'Well, I'm entitled to mine too. Like I said, you asked for what you got just now. O.K., you're a dishy little number and I could find myself going overboard for you in quite a way—but you're not the only girl around, get that into your head! I never had to force a girl yet—I don't get my fun that way—nor have I ever had to beg, and I don't mean to start with you. You'll make a good P.A., I can see that—and that's what you'll be to me. You don't have to worry! I'm not going to spend lonely nights weeping for you, if that's what you think.'

'That's *not*——' Flair began in exasperation; but her words were interrupted by a slam of a door somewhere in the house and a cheerful voice calling her name. She gave Luke an agonised glance and he let go of her arm; and at the same moment Jeff Pattison came striding through the patio door, smiling at them both.

'Ah, you're getting to know each other,' he exclaimed. 'That's good. Flair, you look cold, have you been swimming? Luke, have you had a drink?'

'Not yet, Dad,' Flair answered quickly. 'He— we—there hasn't been time. Yes, I am a bit cold, I'll just go and get dressed—won't be long.' And, acutely conscious of Luke Seager's bright, amused eyes, she escaped and made her way hurriedly to her room to shower again and slip back into slacks and shirt.

But before she did anything at all, she sank down

on her bed, wrapping the towel tightly around her shuddering body, her mind and body in turmoil.

Luke Seager, she thought. *Lucifer*. . . . And Jean's words came back to her again, insistent, inexorable. *They say once he's kissed you, you're branded for life. You'll never be free of him again.* . . .

CHAPTER TWO

FLAIR was in command of herself when she came out again to the patio to find her father and Luke enjoying cool beers. She shook her head as her father offered to fetch her a drink, and collected a Martini and lemonade, dropping several ice-cubes into it. Then she joined the men, stretching herself casually in a sunlounger on the other side of her father from Luke Seager; avoiding, though acutely aware of his sardonic gaze.

'Luke's been telling me about his present assistant,' Jeff remarked, touching her glass with his. 'The one you're replacing. He didn't have time to tell you, I gather, but it seems she's had some kind of accident. I haven't heard the details yet.'

'Broke her leg, poor kid,' Luke supplied wryly. 'Hanging curtains in her new home, of all things—fell off a step-ladder. Of course, she won't be on her feet for a couple of months, which takes care nicely of the months' notice she was going to work for me plus the fortnight extra she was willing to stay to ease you into the job.' Flair felt him glance past her father at her, but she stared at her glass, refusing to meet his eyes. It was all too plain what was coming, and she experienced a sudden feeling of being caught in a trap. How *could* she go and work for Luke Seager, after what had just happened? And without even a month's grace in which to get to know her

father and find her own feet in this strange country.
Yet how could she refuse?

'What do you think, Flair?' Jeff asked, obviously
realising as well as she did what Luke was about to
ask. 'It'd mean starting work more or less straightaway—no time for that holiday we promised ourselves. But there'd be a chance for that later on.
Luke's a good employer, so they tell me.' His eyes
twinkled and Flair wondered just how much Jeff
actually knew about Luke Seager. Did he, for
instance, know of his reputation with women . . .?

She glanced across at Luke and met again that
penetrating blue gaze. There was a quality of challenge about it—as if he were daring her to refuse.
Resist me if you can, it said—*if* you can. And she
felt her blood rise to the challenge. Her eyes locked
with his and it was as if they spoke to each other
without need for words, as if with their eyes they
could say all that was necessary. All right, her green
eyes said to his blue: all right, I'll take your challenge. I'll resist. My mind is set on higher things,
Luke Seager. Whatever other women may say;
whatever brand Lucifer may think he's put upon
me—this time it just isn't going to work. . . .

Luke dropped his gaze as if satisfied, and the
moment of communication passed, leaving Flair
strangely exhilarated. She turned back to Jeff and
found him watching her almost with anxiety; and,
touched by the look on his thin, tired face, she smiled
warmly at him.

'So long as it's all right with you, Dad,' she told him,
'I'm ready to start work straightaway. Only——'
she glanced provocatively at her prospective em

ployer '—I'd like just to have this weekend free, if I may? To get my bearings—get over any jet-lag I may have—that sort of thing? Unless you can't wait . . .?'

She heard a tiny intake of breath from Luke and knew that her shaft had gone home. But he made no other sign; merely inclined his burnished head and said casually: 'No problem at all. I'll expect you on Monday morning, then, about eight? Jeff will make sure you know the way.' He stood up, uncoiling his lithe body with an action that reminded Flair of a tightly-wound spring suddenly loosened. 'Thanks for the beer, Jeff. I'll have to be away now.'

'Oh, surely——' Jeff protested, making to get up too '—you'll be stopping for a bit of lunch?'

Luke shook his head. 'Can't, I'm afraid. Busy man till I get my new assistant!' He glinted a look at Flair. 'Better get plenty of rest between now and Monday,' he advised. 'You'll find you need all your energy—being my personal assistant can be a very demanding position, I'm told!' He paused to watch with amusement as flags of colour mounted in Flair's cheeks, then nodded at Jeff. 'Be seeing you.' He swung on his heel and was gone; and it was as if he left a vast empty space behind him.

Slowly, Flair sank back into her sunlounger and sipped at her Martini. There was no doubt about it, Luke Seager was the most vital, the most compelling and—she had to admit it—the most devastatingly attractive man she had ever met. The memory of that kiss still made her stomach twist, while a vein of fire ran through her body, down her arms and into the palms of her hands when she thought of the way

he'd held her. If she were going to work for him, to
find herself in close contact with him every day, she
was going to have to guard very carefully against
that almost overpowering attraction.

But she could do it, she told herself firmly. No
man had ever found the path to her heart yet, and
there was no way Luke Seager was going to be the
first. If the day ever did come when she gave herself
to a man, it wouldn't be a man like him—a rake, a
demon who branded every attractive woman he
touched. So there was a streak of sensuality in her
that she had never suspected—well, that could be
controlled. *Had* to be controlled, she thought with a
small shiver; or she would be lost. . . .

There was a heavy shower of rain falling when Flair
woke on Monday morning, and she stood at the kitchen window watching it in some dismay. Jeff,
coming in for a cup of tea, smiled and said reassuringly: 'Don't look so worried—it won't last long.
That's one thing about rain out here—it comes down
in a torrent when it does come, but it never lasts.
You'll see, in ten minutes or so the sun'll be shining
again.'

Flair poured some bran flakes into a bowl and
added milk.

'It's just that I'd have liked a fine day to start my
new job—silly, really, but it seems a better omen.'

'Look, you'll be fine. I don't know what you're so
nervous about. Your qualifications are good, you've
got experience in some of the best London hotels—
what's the problem?'

'Oh, I don't know,' said Flair with a shrug. 'Yes,

I suppose it's silly. I just get the feeling that English qualifications and experience in English hotels won't cut much ice with Luke Seager. He'll want things done *his* way—which is fair enough, provided he gives me a chance to find out what that is.'

'Well, of course he will. Luke's not an unreasonable man.' Jeff looked at his daughter, then came over to lay a hand on her shoulder. 'You seem to be making him into some kind of ogre,' he said gently. 'Don't. Luke's a big man, a wealthy man—but he hasn't always been. He had a tough childhood—his father made a real mess of running the two hotels he left Luke and the boy had to put all he had into it just to break even. Nobody ever expected him to make it like he has. He knows what it is to come up from the bottom, Flair.'

'Yes, I know. It's just—oh well, you're right, I'm letting things get on top of me.' She turned away and rinsed her cup at the sink. 'Well, Dad, thanks for a really lovely weekend—I just wish we could have had longer. But we'll promise ourselves that holiday later on, won't we?' She reached up and kissed his thin face. 'Look after yourself, Dad. I'll see you tonight.'

Giving him a bright smile, she picked up her bag and slipped out through the kitchen door to the car-port where the small car stood that her father had bought for her to use during her stay. Flair had objected that it wasn't necessary, she could buy her own car—but she had quickly realised that this was something he wanted to do and that he would be hurt if she insisted. And as she drove it away, follow-ing the route Jeff had shown her the day before into the city of Perth, she reflected that in some way her father seemed particularly vulnerable just now. As if he was suddenly regretting the lost years between them. And she knew that, whatever it cost her, she would do a lot to avoid hurting him.

And if that meant fighting off Luke Seager every minute of every day and still holding on to her job, just to please her father who so plainly thought the world of the younger man, then that—she told herself grimly—was just what she would have to do. . . .

Nobody, for some reason, had prepared Flair for the size and sophistication of the Seager Hotel. In spite of all she had heard about Luke Seager, in spite of her own impression of him, she had still carried the picture in her mind of a medium-sized, mediocre kind of place struggling to make a name for itself, perhaps even succeeding in this faraway country, but with little hope of matching up to the great London hotels in which she had worked. The tall, slender building just off St George's Terrace came therefore as a surprise; the surprise was bigger still when she walked into the foyer and took in the sheer grace and luxury that prevailed even here.

'Miss Pattison?' the svelte receptionist said. 'Yes, Mr Seager is expecting you. You're to go straight to his office suite.' She glanced across the foyer and a uniformed page hurried over. 'Miss Pattison, for Mr Seager,' the girl said, with a friendly smile at Flair, and the page led her over to the lift.

Everywhere Flair looked that morning the same air of quiet luxury and discreet good taste prevailed. It was clear that Seager Hotels aimed only for the

moneyed client. Yet there was no flamboyance, none
of the brashness she had half-expected from Luke
Seager. He must have very good advisers, she
thought as she followed the page from the lift and
along a deeply-carpeted corridor. Good interior
designers as well as a good architect.

Luke Seager's own penthouse suite did nothing to
dispel this impression. As she entered, she was
momentarily arrested by the huge window with its
panoramic view over the Swan River. Forgetting
everything else, she went forward, gazing with
delight at the blueness of the water, dancing with
coloured sails, and the grace of the Narrows Bridge
with King's Park rising steeply beyond; while from
another window she found herself looking almost
directly along St George's Terrace, with the rest of
Perth and its suburbs spread around it.

'Like it?'

The soft drawl startled her; she had thought the
room empty when she entered. Swinging round, she
saw Luke Seager standing near the door, a cynical
smile touching his firm lips. She felt herself blush as
her eyes travelled over him, all too aware that he
was examining her just as closely, yet unable to
glance away until she had taken in every detail of
his appearance; the neat business suit that did
nothing to hide his essential masculinity, the breadth
of his shoulders, the easy grace of his body as he
rested lightly on the balls of his feet like an athlete
ready for the gun.

For a moment she wished that she had not worn
the clinging lawn dress of pale sea-green that so
effectively set off her auburn hair and reflected the

colour of her eyes. She felt suddenly convinced that
it was too low-cut, the wrapover bodice too revealing. Luke's eyes were lingering appreciatively on her
curves, and she knew that he must be remembering
the picture she had presented in her wet bikini
by the swimming-pool. Embarrassed, she turned
away—then remembered her determination that
Luke Seager was never to know the effect he had on
her—never even to be aware that he had any effect
at all. With a tremendous effort, she controlled her
breathing and turned back.

'It's a wonderful view, Mr Seager,' she said sincerely. 'Dad took me driving all around Perth at the
weekend and I can certainly see why they say the
Swan is the most beautiful estuary in the world. I've
never seen anything lovelier.'

His smile widened, but whether from irony or
appreciation of her words she couldn't tell. He
moved across the room and stood beside her, point-
ing out various landmarks. Flair felt her skin tingle
as his arm brushed hers, but she stood still and hoped
that he couldn't hear the sudden thumping of her
heart.

'And now to work,' he said at last, turning away
from the window. 'I understand from your father
that you've had experience in various London hotels.
That should help you—but you'll have to remember
that this isn't London, or even England. We have
our own ways of doing things—I have *my* own ways
of doing things—and we don't like to have them
dismissed as second-rate just because they're not
English.'

'I wouldn't dream——' Flair began, but he went

on as if she hadn't spoken.

'It's a habit some of you Britishers have. Now, we're at a pretty busy time here. There's the Perth Seager, the Melbourne Seager and a few smaller hotels that I'm building up—we'll go into all that thoroughly. Added to those are the leisure centre and hotel I'm building on Blue Island, and the Seager Motel down on the Albany road. Your father's starting on the designs for that one any time now. That adds up to a lot of work, and I hope you're up to it, Flair.'

'I think I am, Mr Seager,' Flair said stiffly, and he cut her short with an impatient gesture.

'I told you, skip the formality. It's Luke and Flair, right? Now, I'm ready to make allowances seeing that you're fresh out from England, but if you don't think you can cope, better say so here and now. Your father seems to think you can, though what he'd know about it I'm not too sure, seeing the time it is since he saw you, and you were only a kid then. But I've got a lot of time for Jeff Pattison, so I'm ready to give you a chance if that's the way you want it.'

He paused and looked at her. Flair met his eyes steadily, though inside she was seething with fury at his patronising manner and abrupt words. *If she didn't think she could cope*, indeed! *Give her a chance*— why, for two pins she'd ram his rotten job down his throat and walk out on him without so much as another word! In fact, she was strongly tempted to do so. And then she remembered Jeff, and knew that she couldn't. For his sake, she had to give it a try at least. If the whole thing did prove to be impossible later on, she could always resign. But she couldn't

turn the job down without having given it—and
Luke Seager, she reluctantly acknowledged—a fair
trial.

'That's the way I want it,' she replied quietly, her
eyes still locked with his. 'I'm ready to give it a
chance too.' That should indicate that she wasn't
here to be bullied, she thought, watching with satisfaction as his eyes narrowed fractionally. But he
wasn't finished yet.

'And——?' he prompted, then when she looked
blank: 'I'm accustomed to being given a name now
and then.'

Flair took a deep breath. 'I'm ready to give it a
chance too,' she repeated, adding reluctantly,
'Luke.' And felt a queer, unexpected thrill as her
mouth shaped his name. She turned away quickly
from the look in his eyes and stared unseeingly out
of the window as he remarked softly: 'That's better.'
Then, more briskly, he began to outline the day's
activities and Flair realised that with the sheer bulk
of work he expected her to get through there was
going to be little time for introspection.

And that, she reflected later as she sat at her own
desk in an adjoining office with papers already piling
up in front of her, was probably just as well.

Rather to Flair's surprise, she settled in well at the
Seager Hotel. There were, of course, differences in
her work here and her experiences in England, but
she soon adapted to them and kept quiet about those
she didn't approve of. As both her father and Luke
had pointed out in their different ways, she was the
stranger here—the foreigner, almost—and when in

Rome it was as well to do as Rome did. In fact, her criticisms were few and she found herself enjoying her work and making friends among the staff.

During the first week or two, she saw little of Luke. Once satisfied that she could cope, he spent most of his time in making visits to the other, smaller hotels he had acquired in and around Perth—hotels not yet of a standard to be dignified with the name Seager Hotel, and probably never to be large enough to be so designated, but still to be improved and stamped with the Seager brand. Flair knew that Luke wanted to make a thorough round of each of these smaller hotels in preparation for a visit to the Blue Island complex and the Albany motel. She wondered whether she would be expected to accompany him on these visits and, in spite of her resolution, felt a tingle of excitement at the idea. Sternly, she repressed it, telling herself that it would be interesting to see some different parts of Western Australia. After all, the trips would be strictly business. . . .

It was while she was thinking about this one morning that she was interrupted by the secretary, Janet, who looked nervously through the door and said: 'Oh, Flair, there's a lady to see Mr Seager.'

'Luke's not here, Janet,' said Flair, glancing up. 'He's over in Fremantle. Anything I can do?'

'I'm not sure——' Janet began, but she was interrupted by a cool voice from behind; a voice that was recognisably American, languidly amused, and that for some reason immediately caused Flair's hackles to rise.

'Don't worry, Janet, I'll wait in his suite,' the voice

said. 'Luke won't mind. He's due back in an hour anyway.'

You know more than I do, then, Flair thought, half rising from her seat as the newcomer entered. She gave a quick startled look at the tall, beautiful brunette, then nodded reassuringly at Janet. 'It's all right, Janet. I'll look after Miss——?'

'Ryan,' the American girl drawled. 'Roxanne Ryan. Luke will have told you about me, I'm sure.' She swayed into the room as Janet closed the door, bringing a waft of heavy perfume with her, and stood looking down at Flair in a way that Flair found maddeningly condescending. 'So you're the new assistant! From England, aren't you? That's fascinating—I'm longing to see England some time. All those *quaint* thatched cottages and shepherds in smocks! You must tell me all about it one day.'

'Of course, Miss Ryan,' Flair said politely. 'When we both have time. Was there anything particular you wanted to see Luke about? Anything I can help with?'

A twitch of amusement showed on the brunette's tanned, flawless features. 'Something particular, yes. Something you can help with—no, I wouldn't really think so. It's rather more personal business that I have with Luke.'

'I see.' Flair found her dislike of the other girl growing. She looked at the tall shapely figure now standing by the window, gazing out over the Swan. She wondered who this exotic creature was, where she had come from; what was her connection with Luke. Clearly, whoever she was, she wasn't short of money; Flair could well appreciate the quality of her Italian silk suit in emerald green patterned with dark blue and the high-heeled gold sandals that so superbly set off her long, well-shaped legs. And she had the looks to carry off the somewhat startling colours, too; her skin tanned a deep gold, dark flashing eyes topped by a cloud of near-black hair, her figure statuesque and voluptuous. Presumably she was one of Luke's girlfriends, Flair thought, suppressing an inexplicable pang at the idea. Well, they'd make a good match, she had to admit that. Together, they couldn't look anything short of stunning.

Roxanne swung round suddenly from the window, her hair billowing like smoke around her classic features, and Flair immediately lowered her eyes. She felt the other girl's stare and her lips tightened.

'What's your name?' the American demanded. 'I don't think Luke ever mentioned it.'

'Flair Pattison. I've only been here a couple of weeks.'

She looked up again and met the dark eyes. They were watching her with an enigmatic expression— almost, she thought, as if their owner were unsure of something. But that couldn't be so—she'd never met anyone so sure of themselves as Roxanne Ryan. Except Luke Seager himself, of course.

'Your father's Jeff Pattison, is that right?'

Flair nodded. 'I've come out on a long visit and wanted to get some further experience in hotel-keeping.'

Roxanne's deep brown eyes narrowed and her lip lifted in a delicate but unmistakable sneer. 'And perhaps to catch a rich hotelier?'

'Catch a——? I'm afraid I don't know what you mean, Miss Ryan.'

'Oh, don't go all English and prissy on me. You know full well what I mean. O.K., so your daddy's done some work for Luke, some good work too, so he tells me. So you've trained in hotel work. So this looks like a good chance, doesn't it? Come out here—worm your way into a job as his P.A.—and you know what they say. Marry the boss. It all fits in, doesn't it?'

Flair sat rigid with anger. Controlling her voice with difficulty, she said: 'No, it does *not* fit in, Miss Ryan! For one thing, I don't think that way. For another, I've no intention of marrying *anyone*—and if I had, it wouldn't be Luke Seager! I can't think of anything worse—I wouldn't marry him if he were the last man between me and the penguins!' She took a deep breath and added: 'I really can't think why you should suggest these things, Miss Ryan—unless perhaps you wanted the job yourself?'

Roxanne took a step forward, her smooth face distorted with anger, but before anything else could happen the office door, which Janet hadn't fully closed, swung open and Luke's voice said cheerfully: 'Now, now, girls, don't fight over me. I'm really not worth it.' And as they both whirled to stare at him, he gave them an impudent grin that brought the blood singing to Flair's cheeks as she realised that he must have heard most, if not all, of her last words.

Discomfited, she dropped her eyes and fiddled with the papers on her desk. But Roxanne was not so easily disturbed. She recovered herself with a speed that Flair had to admire, and flung herself across the room and into his arms.

'Luke! Darling, you're early—maybe that's because you knew little old me would be here waiting for you,' she crooned, lifting her face to his. 'Honey, it seems an age since I saw you. You don't know how slowly the time passes—or maybe you do, huh?'

Flair glanced up from her papers and caught Luke's eye. For a long moment—or maybe it was only seconds—they stared at each other. Then, deliberately and sensually, he gathered Roxanne close against him. He bent his lips to hers and kissed her—a long, intimate kiss, the kind of kiss that doesn't need an audience. His hands moved lingeringly over Roxanne's curves. And Flair, impelled by an overpowering need to be away from their presence, rose quickly to her feet, gathered up a few papers, and stalked with all the dignity she could muster into the tiny room where she kept her typewriter.

She closed the door and leaned against it, her eyes closed. But the image of Luke and Roxanne persisted. And after a few moments, gathering herself as if she were marching into battle, she sat down at the desk, put a sheet of paper in the typewriter and began to pound the keys.

It didn't really matter what she typed. But later, when she found the sheet and looked at it, she was totally baffled by the jumble of meaningless letters that covered its surface.

Luke and Roxanne had gone when Flair finally returned to her office. Presumably they had gone to lunch, though for all she knew they might as easily still be in the suite, in Luke's private quarters; eating together in the small, exquisite dining-room, for instance, or relaxing in the spacious lounge. Or even, she admitted reluctantly, in the bedroom—which Flair herself hadn't even seen but could well imagine. It would be as luxurious as the rest of the hotel, stamped with Luke's own particular sensual masculinity; like sleeping in a jungle, she thought, with an especially dangerous tiger by your side. . . .

She had almost given up any hope of seeing Luke again that day when he returned, his appearance reminding her again unavoidably of the tiger as he came through the door like a great cat on the prowl. He had a glow of satisfaction about him, too; wherever he and Roxanne had been, Flair thought, he'd certainly had the cream. . . . She stood up abruptly as he approached her and backed away towards the small office.

'I was just about to leave, Mr Seager,' she said, her voice tight. 'I'll just tidy up my papers. Unless there's anything else you want?'

Immediately, as Luke Seager's eyes narrowed and roamed up and down the length of her body, she wished she hadn't said that. But all he said, after a nod that might have meant anything, was: 'That's fine, Flair. You get off as soon as you can. I meant to ring and tell you to go early, anyway.' He paused, while Flair wondered what was coming next. 'You'll be making an early start tomorrow, after all,' he went on levelly. 'I want to make that trip to Blue Island we've talked about.'

Flair stared at him. 'Blue Island? *Tomorrow?*'

'Yeah, why not?' His drawl was always more pronounced when he was amused and, to her irritation, he seemed often to be amused by her. 'There's no reason why we shouldn't take off. Nothing urgent to do here, is there?'

'No, but—well, couldn't you have given me more warning?' she asked. 'I mean, springing it on me like this—I might have all sorts of plans, social engagements, anything. I——'

'And have you?' he enquired. 'Plans, social engagements? I didn't realise you'd got such an active social life going in the—what is it?—fortnight you've been here.'

'Well, no, I haven't,' she admitted. 'But that's not the point——'

'It's the only point that concerns me. Look, if it wasn't for your circumstances with your father I'd be wanting you to live in here, Flair. My last P.A. did, and it'd be a damn sight more convenient if you did too. So don't say I haven't made allowances. But all the same, time's money to me and if I say I want to take a trip somewhere and need you along, then I expect you to be free to come, get it? So when you start this hectic social whirl you're obviously expecting to get going, you just remember that and plan accordingly, O.K.?'

'I see!' Flair exclaimed. 'You pay me a salary and that means you've bought me body and soul. I do apologise—I didn't notice that clause in my contract.'

The startling blue of his eyes darkened at that, and he took a step towards her. Flair, alarmed, moved quickly but he moved faster. His hand caught her wrist and held it painfully and he drew her closer, his eyes like ice in the sunburnt face. Flair turned her head away, determined not to meet his gaze, but his other hand came up to force her chin round. She wanted to close her eyes but was afraid of what might happen if she did. Already she was aware of the wild jerking of her heart, the heat of her quickened blood, the tremors that were threatening to make her legs give way beneath her. As Luke drew her even nearer, she was aware of her breasts brushing against his hard chest, the nipples already taut and tingling. With her free hand, she pushed desperately against him, but it was like trying to shift a wall of rock. She opened her mouth to protest; but before she could utter a word he had fastened his own lips on hers, keeping them apart and exploring the crevices of her mouth, while his hand slid down from her chin, encircling her neck, caressing her throat and finally describing a series of tiny circles as it progressed down to the neck of her blouse.

When he finally removed his mouth from hers, Flair was weak and dizzy, and in no condition to struggle. Indeed, she felt that if he were to let her go she must fall. She leaned against him, breathless, bemused, unable either to move or speak. She felt Luke move slightly away and looked up dazedly to find him watching her almost with the expression of a scientist absorbed in an experiment.

'I——' she whispered, but he cut in smoothly.

'Do you think I've bought you body and soul now, Flair Pattison?' he mused. 'Maybe I don't need to buy . . . maybe you'd rather give? But I won't ask that of you—not yet. Not until you're ready. . . .' He

gathered her against him again and his lips found
her eyelids, closing them with tiny kisses that sent
shivers through her whole body. She felt a tiny trail
of fire as his mouth moved away to her ears, nipping
gently at each lobe, then under the line of her chin
to the hollow of her throat. She was barely aware
that he had let go of her wrist, that his arms encircled
her completely, nor even that her own arms had
slipped up round his neck. There was nothing in the
world at this moment but herself and Luke Seager
. . . the man no woman could resist. . . . Not even
Flair Pattison. . . .

A sudden wave of scent assailed her nostrils and
the image of Roxanne Ryan swayed unwanted into
her mind. Roxanne—surely that was *her* scent, waft-
ing up from Luke's shirtfront. It was only hours since
he'd been with her. Brought brutally back to earth,
Flair wrenched herself away, taking him by surprise
this time so that he let her go with a suddenness that
had them both stumbling. Taking advantage of the
moment, Flair retreated behind her desk, the door
to the small office behind her, and glared at her
employer.

'Don't come near me again!' she panted, green
eyes wide under the dishevelled auburn hair. 'Don't
touch me again—ever!' She couldn't add: *especially
when you've been with* her *all afternoon*—he'd be bound
to put the wrong interpretation on it. Vainly, she
cast about for something else to say, but Luke saved
her the trouble.

'What's the matter now?' he demanded, advanc-
ing on her. 'You were *enjoying* that, enjoying it just as
much as I was. So why stop? We're both adult

people, aren't we? Is there something wrong about us making love? Something evil? Don't go all moral on me—not in this day and age!'

'It's nothing to do with that,' Flair snapped. 'I just don't want to—to have affairs. Is there something wrong with *that?* Something unnatural? I told you, I'm not interested in that kind of thing. I want a career—that's not so unusual, is it? And as far as I'm concerned, careers and marriage don't mix. Not yet, anyway—not until I've got a lot further than I am now.'

'My God,' he said slowly, 'you do take things to heart, don't you? Whoever mentioned marriage? I was talking about pleasure, that's all—natural, healthy, wholesome fun.'

'Well, that's not my idea of fun, then,' she retorted. 'Yes, if you like, I do equate sex with marriage. I thought *that* was normal. So until I get married—if I ever do—I'm not having anything to do with sex. It makes life too complicated.'

'But what a complication,' he murmured. 'And boy, what a load of trouble you're storing up for yourself, Flair honey. No marriage—so no sex. It'll never work—not with a bundle of dynamite like you. And if you ask if there's something unnatural in not wanting what every healthy man and woman in the world wants, well, I have to tell you, I think there is. Something very unnatural. But you'll find out. It's my guess you haven't even begun to realise your own potential.' He walked to the door, and Flair closed her eyes again rather than watch the sinuous movements of the body that had only moments ago been pressed so closely and intimately to hers. At the door, he paused and his brilliant blue gaze met hers mockingly.

'Don't forget what I said about an early start, Miss Pattison,' he murmured. 'And bring your tooth-brush, won't you—we'll be staying over.'

CHAPTER THREE

BLUE ISLAND lay off the coast a few miles north of
Perth. Smaller than the popular holiday island of
Rottnest, it nevertheless had great potential, as Luke
explained on the way to the beach where he kept his
motor-launch. He intended to develop it on similar
lines to the Seager Hotels, with the added attractions
of a health farm, together with gymnasium, squash
and tennis courts and various other outdoor activities. There were sufficient inlets on the sheltered
side of the island for plenty of beaches, one or two
of them secluded enough to be used for naturist
bathing, and there were deep pools ideal for skin-
diving.

'Naturist beaches had a sticky time of it when they
were first established around Perth,' Luke remarked,
helping Flair into the launch and showing her where
to sit. 'But they've come to be accepted, and the
ones I've earmarked on Blue Island won't offend
anyone.' He glanced sideways at Flair, his eyes
twinkling. 'Maybe we could try them out while we're
over there.'

The roar of the engine drowned Flair's reply, but
she knew that the flush on her face must tell him
just how she felt about *that* suggestion. Nude
bathing indeed—and with him! There was nothing
she was less likely to do—well, almost nothing. Still
scarlet, she turned to look out to sea and the dark

smudge that was Blue Island.

'You don't seem keen on the idea,' Luke persisted as the engine quietened and the launch began the run across the bay. Flair bit her lip. Sitting where she was—where *he'd* told her to sit—she felt uncomfortably close to him. His thigh brushed against hers; unnecessarily, she thought, but she could hardly ask him to remove it. She shifted a little in her seat and caught his bright, mocking glance on her immediately.

'Ever been bathing in the altogether?' he enquired. 'There's nothing like it—the feeling of the water flowing over your body, completely unrestricted. And as for sunbaking—so long as you don't overdo it, of course. That can be very painful indeed!'

He was laughing at her, it was quite obvious, and Flair determined not to rise to the bait. But Luke wasn't going to let her get away with it so lightly.

'Of course, I forgot, that kind of thing doesn't interest you,' he commented, keeping a light hand on the steering of the boat. 'You're the single-minded career girl, aren't you? The human body's just a necessary encumbrance—though a very decorative one in your case, I admit.' His glance was now frankly appreciative, flicking over her body as he took in the pale blue slack suits, set off by a plain white shirt and a scarf in darker blue silk. 'Seems a shame it'll never enjoy the pleasures it's so obviously made for.'

'Mr Seager,' Flair said through tight lips, 'I've told you before how I feel about—about that kind of thing. Can't we just give it a rest?'

'Funny the way you always call me Mr Seager when we get to talking about sex,' he mused. 'Almost as if you were scared of something. Of me, maybe? Or . . . even of yourself?' His own lips twitched with amusement as he watched her face flame.

'We're *not* talking about sex!' she managed at last. 'At least, I'm not—you seem to think and talk of nothing else. I can't understand how you ever found the time to build up a hotel business!'

'Oh, now that's not fair,' he protested. 'You know how hard I work. But I like to play too. Isn't a man entitled to a little fun now and then?'

'Oh yes, by all means. But not with me!' she shot at him. 'If that's all you're going to Blue Island for, you brought the wrong person. You should have asked Roxanne to accompany you—I'm sure she'd have been glad to take a few notes, among any other little tasks you might have in mind!'

For a moment she thought she had gone too far. His eyes hardened to the colour of slate as he stared at her. Then, with a soft sound that might have meant anything, he turned abruptly away, leaving Flair to regain control of her breathing and, after a few minutes, to look around her.

The scene was incredibly beautiful. Behind them now lay the coast of Western Australia, a strip of dazzlingly white sand with the rainbow colours of the bush, alive with wildflowers, stretching behind. The tower blocks of Perth shimmered down the coast and she could see a liner making its way to the busy port of Fremantle.

Ahead, islands were strewn in a long chain. In the morning sunshine they looked like a glowing neck-

lace of opals. But she knew that they could be
treacherous; the early days had seen many wrecked
ships here, some of them still visible in the clear,
deadly waters. Caught in the storms that could rage
along this coast, struggling to pick a way between
the rocks that sprang like jagged teeth to tear at
whatever might come near, many of the pioneer
ships had foundered off this coast when exploration
had first begun. And later, as the settlers searching
for a better life had undertaken the vast and dangerous journey from the other side of the world, more
than one ship with a cargo of wives and children,
and household effects from tubs and mangles to
grand pianos and even the occasional carriage, so
useless in this wild country, had gone to the bottom
within sight of the Australian shores.

Blue Island was one of the innermost islands of
the chain, sheltered from the worst of the Indian
Ocean's tumult by the curve of the coast and the
islands that lay outside it. Flair watched with interest
as Luke brought the launch close to it, and leaned
forward excitedly as he took the boat right round
the island so that she could see the entire coastline.
A gasp of delight rose to her lips as she saw the
waters of one bay alive with birds—cormorants and
gulls mostly, accompanied by a flock of pelicans that
rose into the air at the launch's approach, their
ungainly, huge-billed bodies taking on a peculiar
grace as they flapped higher and higher, circling
with lazy movements until they were little more than
dark specks against the immense blue of the sky.

'Oh, how beautiful,' Flair exclaimed softly. 'And
I always thought pelicans were just comic birds.'

Luke grinned abstractedly as he handled the launch through a submerged reef. 'They're ace fliers, pelicans. And I've never been able to see quite why, since their food comes entirely from the sea. Guess it must be sheer joy at being alive.' He turned the boat into a hidden harbour and brought it alongside a wooden jetty. 'Well, here we are. Blue Island— playground of W.A.'

Flair scrambled eagerly ashore and stared about her. The tiny harbour was perfect and could take several boats—allowing both for the hotel launches that would be needed as ferries, and for those guests who would want to bring their own craft. Craggy rocks sheltered it, and on top of the highest was a small lookout station; beyond, the road led to the complex of the hotel block.

'There'll be chalets as well, for those who want to be private,' Luke explained, leading her along the newly-made road. 'You'll notice a few old buildings too—the island was settled once, but of course it was too small to be a realistic idea. Not too small for what I want to do, though—in fact, it's just ideal. Big enough to wander about in, not too big to handle. I've got a lot of ideas for this place.'

As he showed her around, Flair became conscious of a feeling of unease that had been niggling at her ever since their arrival in the harbour. She couldn't quite place what it was—a sensation of something being not quite right, not as she had expected. But it was not until they had completed a circuit of the building work and returned to the hotel itself that it dawned on her just what it was.

'There's no one here,' she said slowly, pausing at

the entrance to the empty foyer. 'Nobody working: nobody at all.' She swung round on Luke Seager. 'Just what's going on?'

'Why, you've just seen for yourself,' he answered sardonically. 'Nothing.'

'No, I mean—you said we'd be—be staying overnight! But there's no one here, no one at all——'

'So you said.' His eyes were bright and mocking. 'So there'll be no one to see just what goes on, will there?' he added in a throaty whisper, and Flair backed away with a gasp of alarm.

Luke roared with laughter. 'Don't be such a terrified little rabbit, Flair! I'm not going to eat you. What did you expect anyway—a hive of industry? You ought to have known there'd be no workmen here. We're waiting for the electrics, aren't we? Come back next week and the place'll be buzzing again.'

'So why didn't we come next week?' she asked, trying to quell the trembling of her voice.

'Because,' he said with a forced gentleness, as if he were talking to an imbecile, 'I wanted to come *now*. I wanted to see the place with nothing happening, get a clear view of it without a lot of workmen running about and getting in the way. There are various things I've got to decide at this stage and I wanted peace and quiet to do it. It *suits* me to have the place to myself for two or three days—otherwise I wouldn't have arranged it that way, believe me!'

Flair did believe him. Luke Seager wasn't the man to let his work be held up a day longer than was necessary. But her mind caught on to something else he had said. Two or three *days*! That meant—nights, as well. Nights alone here with Luke Seager—with no possibility of escape. She swallowed convulsively and said with an effort at nonchalance: 'I see. Well, I hope you've at least made sure there's some food here. And a couple of bedrooms properly furnished.'

His lips lifted in the mocking smile she was becoming used to.

'What do you take me for, Miss Pattison?' he drawled. 'I gave orders for one of the chalets to be specially prepared. We should find everything we need there—except electricity, of course. But there's bottle gas for the fridge and cooker—we'll be comfortable enough.'

'*One* of the chalets?' Flair asked, her voice higher than she meant it to be. 'You—you mean we're sharing?'

'I don't have the time or the money to spare for frills.' His tone was dangerous. 'I told you, it'll be adequate and quite as comfortable as we need. If you don't like it, there are plenty of others. Only of course—they're not furnished. But it's entirely up to you.'

He turned away and Flair stared speechlessly after him. Common politeness, courtesy, old-fashioned chivalry seemed to mean nothing to this man! But it was no more than she should have expected from him, she thought angrily as she followed him on a tour through the hotel. And she was learning every day just what she *should* expect.

It was dusk before they finished the tour of the hotel. Flair was kept busy making notes as Luke examined each room with a meticulous attention that surprised her; though on reflection she realised that it shouldn't have, since only two weeks in his employ had shown him to be a perfectionist in anything he undertook. If he had a fault in his approach to his business it was that he found it difficult to delegate, though this again was understandable since he seemed to have most skills at his fingertips and certainly wasn't one to suffer fools gladly.

It came as a surprise too to learn that Luke was his own interior decorator—in the main rooms anyway. He had brought with him various books of wallpapers, paint charts and swatches of material as well as carpet and tile samples. Apparently he intended going over all these and roughing out a scheme for the hotel in general, the individual rooms in particular. The size of the task impressed Flair— she could see now why he intended staying several days. Especially if he proposed to work out schemes for the chalets as well.

It was almost too dark to see when Luke finally straightened up and declared that work was over for the day.

'A meal and an early night, I guess,' he decided. 'Daylight's more use than lamplight and until W.A. goes in for daylight saving we'll still get more sun in the morning than the evening, so we'll use it. Now, let's go and see how they've fitted out that chalet. I brought some fresh foods in the icebox on the boat— I'll fetch them once we're settled in and maybe you could knock up a meal.'

It was on the tip of Flair's tongue to refuse, saying that she was his personal assistant, not chief cook and bottle-washer, but she bit the words back, knowing that they would be unreasonable. While she was preparing the meal, Luke could be continuing with his work; it would be foolish to insist that he took his turn with the chores, thus delaying their return to the mainland.

She followed him along the winding path to the chalets. Peppermint trees and eucalyptus grew alongside it, and the scent of wildflowers filled the air. A few nightbirds called and she could hear the muted roar of breakers from the seaward beaches of the island. As they came into the open she looked up and caught her breath at the sight of the sky, aglow with hundreds of thousands of stars, a myriad sparkling needle-points against the velvet bowl of night; so many that for a wild, dizzying moment she felt almost that she could hear them, like music in the heavens. She stood transfixed, unaware until his bare arm brushed hers that Luke was close beside her.

'It's because we're so far away from city lights,' he murmured. 'Nothing to stop us seeing them. Magnificent, isn't it.'

They walked on slowly, still keeping close together. Strangely, Flair felt now none of the electric disturbance that his presence had caused her before. Here on the island, under the stars, there was a rightness about their silent companionship that she wouldn't have believed possible. Her thoughts returned to the kisses he had given her, beside the swimming-pool and in the office, and this time, instead of shrugging the memories away with anger and outrage, she allowed her mind to dwell on them, reliving the experiences with a pleasure she only half admitted.

The chalets stood dotted among the trees, each secluded in its own right. Luke stopped on the path, checked the key, then led the way to the one where he intended they should spend the night.

Instantly, Flair's contentment evaporated. She stood stock still on the path, staring at the small cottage-like building which Luke expected her to share with him. It was altogether too intimate, she decided with a quiver of pure panic. Yet there was nowhere else fit to sleep, she'd already seen that. And as Luke unlocked the door and called to her to come inside she followed slowly.

He was lighting a portable gas-lamp when she entered, and the soft glow filled the room with a cosiness she hadn't expected. Interested in spite of herself, she glanced around, approving the simple but comfortable furnishings, the airiness of the decor. If this was a prototype, she had to give her approval. She moved about, examining the different features, then followed Luke as he led the way into the small kitchen.

'Is this how they're all to be done out?' she asked, gazing around in delight. 'It's lovely! Almost a real little home. And when the electricity's in. . . .' She wandered back into the lounge room and opened a further door. 'Oh, and here's the bedroom. . . .' Her voice trailed away.

'What's the problem, no bed?' Luke enquired as he came to stand beside her. Together, they stared in the glowing lamplight at the huge double bed with its soft duvet. There was little else in the room; a chest, a fitted wardrobe and vanity unit, an easy chair and a small table at each side of the headboard.

Wordlessly, Flair glanced sideways up at Luke and was aggrieved to see his mouth twitching with amusement.

'There is another bedroom, you know,' he told her, striding across the room to a door at the side. 'See, all mod cons—shower room——' he flung open the door and marched inside, Flair following '—and children's room. All suitably—ah.' His last word dropped like a stone into the silence and Flair saw him bite his lip as if to hide a grin.

'All totally unfurnished,' she finished coldly as they looked at the bare room beyond the shower room. 'Your orders don't seem to have quite got across this time, Luke. Or maybe they did. Maybe you knew about this all along.'

He merely grunted, turning back into the main bedroom and pulling the door closed behind him. Flair watched him, her heart beating fast. It was fully dark outside now—no chance of getting back to the mainland tonight through all those reefs. What were they going to do? Left to Luke, she had a very good idea of what the answer might be and her pulses quickened. But it wasn't going to be like that, she reminded herself. All right, so he was an attractive man—just about the most devastatingly attractive she'd ever set eyes on, she acknowledged bitterly—but she wasn't about to overturn all her principles and ambitions just for the experience of sharing his bed. No way! There had to be some other way round the problem.

'Look,' she said with a calmness that she was far from feeling, 'you can't really expect me to sleep— to share that bed with you.'

His eyes were mocking as he looked her up and down. 'Can't I? Stranger things have happened.'

'No, you *can't*!' she exploded, clenching her fists. 'Surely even you can see how impossible it is——'

'Not at all impossible——'

'—how totally out of the question——'

'What *was* the question, now?'

'—how absolutely unreasonable——'

'Come now, I can think of several very good reasons——'

'—and utterly *crazy* this is!' she panted, determined to finish in spite of his flippant interruptions. 'I'm not even going to argue about it, and that's flat. I am *not* sharing that bed with you—so you'd better find somewhere else to sleep for the night. And tomorrow night and the night after that, if you're determined to stay.'

Luke looked at her. His eyes glittered in the lamplight.

'*I'd* better find somewhere else?' he repeated softly. 'But *I'm* not the one who's objecting to sharing the bed. You are. Therefore it's surely only reasonable that *you* should be the one to seek alternative accommodation. And besides that, it *is* my chalet—or had you forgotten that?'

Flair gazed helplessly at him. He meant what he said; she could see that. He intended to spend the night—every night—in that king-sized bed, with or without her. From the look on his face, it seemed almost as if he wasn't bothered which—but Flair didn't feel like trusting to that impression. Especially when she remembered the wisp of a nightdress she'd brought. Her face aflame, she turned away, assessing the main room somewhat hopelessly.

If only there were some kind of settee or couch, she thought. But there were only two armchairs. Well, they would just have to do. They were both large and well padded. Pulled almost together—perhaps with that footstool in between for extra length—they should make an adequate bed. And Luke Seager would surely realise then that she meant what she said. Until now, she had the uncomfortable feeling that he thought she was merely playing hard to get, with every intention of succumbing when they'd both had enough of the game.

Well, he'd find out his mistake. For Flair, this was no game. She'd seen from her mother's example to what heights single-mindedness—in both senses of the phrase—could take a woman. She intended to scale no less a peak herself.

She said no more about the bed, but went on into the kitchen to prepare a meal while Luke went down to the boat to fetch the ice-box. Their supper had necessarily to be somewhat simple, since the portable gas cooker he had had installed temporarily in the kitchen consisted only of two burners and a grill. But it cooked steaks to perfection, and together with salad, fruit and cheese the meal set out on the screened verandah looked and tasted as appetising as Flair could have wished.

'Very nice indeed,' Luke commented, producing a bottle of wine. 'Well, do you realise this is the inaugural ceremony of Blue Island Leisure Centre? Could be a big thing for Seager Hotels, you know—if this one takes off I've plans for others. This is only a beginning.'

'But can you expand on such a scale?' Flair asked. 'I mean, there's this—the Albany Motel—all your other smaller places, as well as the Seager Hotels themselves. I know they're all making a profit, but can it stand expansion on the scale you're planning? A place like this must take a fortune to get going.'

'Ah, there are ways and means,' Luke told her mysteriously. 'Ways that sometimes even a personal assistant might not know about . . . just yet, anyway. Pass your glass, there's still plenty of wine here.'

Feeling herself blush slightly, Flair did so. Presumably that had been a gentle way of reminding her to mind her own business. Well, if that was the way he wanted it. . . . She leaned back in her chair, gazing up at the stars. There was little to recognise here from the northern skies she was accustomed to seeing. Probably there were familiar constellations if one knew where to look—but most of them were strange to her. She must get a book, learn a little about them. She didn't know a lot about the skies of the northern hemisphere but could pick out the more familiar planets and formations. To be unable to do so here gave her an odd feeling of disorientation.

'Well, I guess it's time for bed,' said Luke, breaking in on her thoughts. 'Put the dishes in soak for now and do them by daylight, I don't want to use too much gas.' He turned his head and she caught the wicked shine of his eyes in the dim light. 'Have you made up your mind where you're going to sleep yet?'

'Oh yes,' she replied lightly. 'I'll use the lounge. I'll be quite all right—you needn't worry your head about me.'

He raised his eyebrows at that, then put out both hands and raised her from her chair. They stood close and she felt a shiver pass down her limbs. She could feel his breath cool on her forehead as she looked up at him.

'Sure you can't be tempted?' he asked softly, and she felt his fingertips slide slowly up the length of her arms, describe minute circles on the rounded point of her shoulders, then slide slowly down again.

Oh God, she thought, if only you knew. . . . But she stiffened her body and answered steadily: 'Quite, thank you.' She moved away and he made no attempt to detain her. 'Shall I use the shower first, or will you?'

'There's an answer to that, too,' he grinned, 'but I guess you wouldn't find it funny. Or interesting. . . . You go first, little ice-maiden. I'll have a last look round out here.'

That wasn't good either, she realised a moment later. It meant he would have to come back through the lounge to reach the bedroom, and after her shower she'd intended being in her nightie. Well, O.K. It could be managed. Quickly she rearranged the chairs, making a bed of sorts with a couple of rugs she found in a cupboard. One of the pillows from the big bed—it really looked quite comfortable, she decided. Adequate, anyway. . . . She hurried through to the shower-room, acutely anxious to get through before he should decide to come in.

It was more than a little inconvenient that she had to pass through the bedroom to get to the shower, she mused, standing under the refreshing spray. And shook herself irritably at the thought that

somehow she'd mismanaged the whole affair. After
all, he *ought* to have been the one to be sleeping on
the chairs. . . . But maybe chivalry wasn't part of the
Australian scene; she'd heard that there was an odd
sort of equality here, with the women allowed to do
most things just as the men did—except for going
into bars, for instance, or joining in the male conversation at a party. She had already been to one
such function and been amused and slightly outraged
by the way the men all congregated at one end of
the room, leaving the women to themselves at the
other. Maybe this was just another example—when
there was only one bed, it automatically became the
male preserve. Unless the female chose to share
it. . . .

Well, that was one thing this female *wasn't* doing.
Flair towelled herself vigorously and stepped out of
the shower compartment. Her flimsy nightie was
hanging on the back of the door and she slipped it
on, wishing rather ruefully that she'd brought
something more substantial—even a pair of pyjamas.
It was hardly protection—though she'd have needed
armour plating to protect herself from Luke Seager
in determined mood, she thought wryly as she
opened the door to the bedroom.

'Hi,' came the familiar drawl before she had time
to blink. 'Have a good shower? You look as if you
did—all pink and delicious.'

Flair closed her eyes in exasperation—then, opening them, realised that Luke was looking with frank
delight at the picture she made in the gossamer
nightie. Hastily she reached for her damp towel and
wound it round her, and Luke laughed.

'Such modesty! And so needless, too. Why hide such beauty?' He moved sinuously across the room and Flair, terrified that he meant to snatch the towel away, clasped it more tightly about her. 'Don't look at me like that, little elf. I've told you before, I don't eat the small ones.' His blue eyes caressed her and her skin tingled. 'You really are an astonishing mixture, Flair Pattison,' he murmured as if to himself. 'Fire and ice aren't in it with you. You say one thing and your body is screaming the exact opposite. And you know, I'm beginning to believe that you don't even realise it.' His fingertips lifted her chin so that he could search her own green eyes, dark as forest pools. 'Do you, Flair? Do you know what you can do to men with one look from under those impossibly long lashes of yours? Do you know what you're saying when you part those soft lips; when you stand in just that way; when you—my God!' He twisted away from her with a sudden inexplicable emotion. 'If I thought you had any real idea, I'd—I'd——'

You'd what? Flair longed to ask. But she kept silent, knowing instinctively that this might drive him just too far, knowing that she would be totally unable to control any subsequent events. Her heart hammered so loudly that she was sure he must hear it. She wanted to run, to get away, as far away as possible, even while her common sense told her there was nowhere to run to. But it wasn't her common sense that kept her rooted to the spot. It was something else—a sheer paralysed inability to move and, somewhere deep inside, a tremulous excitement.

Luke turned back. His face looked suddenly haggard, but no less attractive. He came a step nearer,

laid his hands lightly on her shoulders and looked
gravely down into her face.

'Just answer me this, Flair, and answer it
honestly,' he said quietly. 'Do you really intend
sleeping out there on that Heath Robinson contrap-
tion of chairs you've set up? Or are you just playing?
I'm serious now, Flair. If you want to share the bed,
this is your last chance to say so.'

Afterwards, Flair was proud of the way she didn't
hesitate. Staring straight back at him, her chin lifted
almost in defiance, she answered with a steadiness
that didn't extend to her heartbeat.

'No, I'm not playing,' she told him, a tiny flame
of triumph licking at her taut nerves as she spoke the
words. 'I'm sleeping alone. Tonight—and every
night.'

He continued to probe her eyes with his; then he
dropped his hands and turned away from her. His
face was averted as he said harshly: 'You'd better
go, then. We've got a heavy day tomorrow.' He
didn't look round as Flair, somehow deflated, crept
to the door; nor as she drew it to a close behind her.
And although she lay awake for some time on her
uncomfortable makeshift bed, listening to his movements as he showered and made ready for bed, he
did not—as she had half expected—open the door
and come into her room.

The tiny flame of triumph had died away, a fire
that had never really lived. Flair's dreams, when she
finally—and fitfully—did sleep, were a confused
jumble in which Luke Seager figured largely and
disturbingly. At least twice she woke convinced that
his arms were about her. But when morning came

and she struggled reluctantly to awareness of a new day, she realised fully that he had taken her at her word, and left her severely alone.

But that's what you wanted, she told herself savagely as she rose wearily and made her way to the kitchen for a drink of cool orange juice. Wasn't it?

So why the feeling of regret ... of disappointment ...?

CHAPTER FOUR

A night's restless sleep on a makeshift bed did not, Flair soon realised, prepare one for a day's intensive work on an Australian island. As she sat in the kitchen, sipping slowly at her orange juice, she did feel some strength returning, but knew that she would be fit for very little that day and looked forward with some dread to a second and maybe even a third night on the chairs.

Not that a night in a comfortable king-sized bed seemed to have done much more for Luke. He appeared a few minutes after Flair, looking much as she felt—drawn, hollow-eyed and weary. They might as well have spent the night *his* way, she reflected wryly, if looks were anything to go by! Or perhaps his haggardness was due to the fact that they *hadn't* done so ... much as, if she were honest, she had to admit that hers was. . . .

Shrugging aside that unwelcome thought, she offered him a glass of orange juice and went through to the shower-room, unable to help noticing the tumbled look of the bed as she passed it. It certainly looked as if he had had a restless night—she only wished that she had had as much room in which to toss and turn. Armchairs, she had discovered, however well padded and comfortable for lounging in, were far too restrictive for any length of time.

The shower revived her and she felt more alive

when she was dressed, this time in fresh jeans and loose blue shirt. While Luke showered, she prepared breakfast and while they ate it they discussed the day's work; both, Flair felt, instinctively avoiding any more personal issue. And it continued that way as they went on with their examination of the complex, concentrating today on the bedrooms in the hotel before working through to the gymnasium and games rooms.

Lunch was a snack of rolls and cold chicken, put up by Flair as Luke made his final preparations for the day. As she ate, Flair found herself growing increasingly sleepy. The interest of the morning's work had banished her tiredness; having stopped, she now felt inexpressibly weary, her body aching as if she had been bruised, and a longing for rest swept over her.

'You're just about flat out,' Luke said abruptly, and her head jerked up as she realised he was watching her.

'I'm not,' she denied hastily. 'It's just the sun— it's so much warmer today.'

Luke grunted. 'It'll get a lot warmer than this. This is only spring sunshine. If you're going to find it affecting you this much——'

Flair opened her mouth to deny that it did, then caught his mocking glance and subsided. He had almost trapped her then. Though why she shouldn't admit she was tired wasn't altogether clear to her— except that it might involve them in another argument about the bed and who was to sleep in it that night. And just at present the thought of that huge spread of mattress, topped with its light, cosy duvet,

was almost alluring enough for her to give in, whatever else that might entail. .... She stifled a yawn
and turned her head away from Luke's gaze.

'I'm afraid I can't give you the afternoon off,' he
remarked sardonically, and Flair stiffened.

'I'm not asking you to.'

'It would only mean stretching out our stay here
even longer,' he continued as if she hadn't spoken,
and Flair sighed with exasperation.

'I told you, I'm not asking for time off, I'm perfectly ready to start work again as soon as you are,
and I shall be only too pleased when we can get this
whole job finished and get back to the mainland.
Blue Island Leisure Centre will be very nice, I'm
sure, when it's finished and there are some people
here—just at present it's more than a trifle dull, don't
you find?'

She jumped to her feet and turned to stare defi-
antly down at him, but Luke stayed where he was,
sprawled at ease in the shade of a peppermint tree.
He was dressed in a workmanlike way today, with
faded jeans and a white shirt left unbuttoned almost
to the waist. The hairs on his chest glinted gold
where the sun caught them. He looked up at her, his
eyes the same intense blue as the sky, and she felt a
twinge of annoyance at the mockery in them.

'Dull?' he said thoughtfully, as if the question
needed some cogitation. 'No, I can't say I've found
it dull. Strenuous, perhaps; certainly more than a
mite frustrating. But dull—no, I wouldn't say so.'

'Oh, you're just being deliberately aggravating!'
she exclaimed, turning abruptly away. She heard a
quick movement behind her then and felt an iron

hand on her wrist. Then she was turned, none too gently, and made to face the hard face of her employer.

'Maybe you'd rather I was deliberately something else,' he grated. 'There just isn't any pleasing you, is there, Flair? You don't like it when I'm friendly—you don't like it when I keep things cool. Just what *is* it you want—or don't you even know that?'

'Let me go!' she panted furiously. 'Why do you have to take everything to extremes anyway? Your idea of being friendly goes a lot farther than mine, can't you realise it? Or haven't you ever met a woman who can say no to you? I don't suppose you have,' she went on more slowly, remembering again the words of the woman on the plane. 'They call you Lucifer, don't they? They say when you kiss a woman you brand her for life. They say you're irresistible. Well, you're *not*—because *I* can resist you, and all too easily. And that's what really bugs you, isn't it? It's nothing to do with me, personally. I'm just another conquest, another scalp you want to hang on your belt. And you just can't stand the thought that I might turn out to be the one who got away!'

She almost cried out as Luke's fingers tightened round her wrist, burning the tender flesh. But the look in his eyes silenced her protests. This time, she knew with a twist of fear, she really had overstepped the mark. She was about to experience the full force of his anger—and she quailed at the thought.

But Luke said nothing. His eyes bored into hers, searching out her innermost thoughts until she felt like a snail with its shell stripped from around it. His fingers were bands of iron round her wrist; his face was like stone.

'My God,' he said at last, his voice rough and grating. 'You certainly do get around, don't you? If that's what you manage to pick up in two weeks, what little titbits are you going to have gathered in a month—a year? Just where do you get these tasty little items from, anyway?'

'I don't go around gossiping, if that's what you mean,' Flair retorted, some of her courage returning. 'And it's hardly my fault if you get gossiped about, anyway. Maybe you ought to be more careful what you do, if you don't want talk. There's a saying that there's no smoke without fire, or haven't you heard it?'

'I've heard it,' he gritted. 'And I'd still like to know where you picked up that faradiddle you were kind enough to repeat just now.'

'As a matter of fact,' she said icily, 'I heard it before I even landed in Perth. From a perfect stranger—a woman who sat beside me on the plane. And she'd never met you—it just seemed to be common knowledge.'

'I see.' Abruptly, he let go of her wrist and Flair backed away rubbing it tenderly. 'And, naturally, you believed it. Took it all in, all wide-eyed and innocent. And then decided to teach me a lesson, perhaps? Teach me that I wasn't God's gift to womankind?'

'Nothing of the sort,' Flair said weakly, uncomfortably aware that this was very much the tenor of her thoughts over the past few days. 'I told you, I'm——'

'Not interested in that kind of thing,' he finished for her. 'The single-minded career girl—or maybe just a foolish virgin. Well, whichever it is, Miss Pattison, we'd better get back to work, don't you think? Or you're going to be incarcerated here with me for even longer than I'd planned. And neither of us would enjoy that . . . would we?'

At the patronising tone in his voice, Flair's fingers clawed instinctively and she ached to hit him. But the memory of his hand around her wrist prevented her; she wasn't at all sure that Luke's code included not hitting a woman. A shiver touched her spine at the thought of what rousing him to real fury might entail, and she turned away, picking up her notebook from where it lay and making a supreme effort to become the cool, efficient personal assistant.

Neither of them spoke much more that day, except about the work in hand. Luke drove them both mercilessly to get as much done as possible and Flair would have protested had she not known that he was as exhausted as she was. In any case, she knew that it would only lead to further argument. But there was more than one occasion on which her thoughts turned with longing to that big comfortable bed.

At last dusk fell and Luke declared work over for the day. Wearily, they retraced their steps to the chalet. Almost too tired to care about food, Flair opened the fridge and stared inside. She felt Luke close behind her and stiffened; but to her astonishment, he said only in a curiously gentle voice:

'Go and put your feet up, Flair. I'll deal with supper.'

'But——'

'Do as you're told,' he said with mock severity. 'I'm capable of grilling a steak and washing a bit of lettuce, you know.'

Flair hesitated for one more brief second, then gave in gratefully and sank into one of the armchairs. Her mind was too dulled to think; she merely lay there, her feet on the footstool, staring blankly at the opposite wall. Presently the aroma of grilling steak floated out from the kitchen, but Flair didn't smell it. Thankfully, easily, she had fallen asleep.

She was only half aware of Luke coming into the room with two plates; only dimly realised that she was roused enough to eat a few mouthfuls and drink a glass of wine. Then she was drifting away again. And smiling in her dreams as she thought she felt strong arms lift her as if she were a baby, carry her into the other room and lay her gently on the bed. Barely conscious but revelling in the longed-for comfort, she spread herself out on the mattress, snuggled under the duvet, and slept soundly then throughout the night.

The chattering of a flight of Twenty-Eight parrots brought Flair back to consciousness the next morning. The light was just beginning to filter through the curtains. She opened her eyes slowly, aware of the refreshing feel of having enjoyed a good night's sleep. And then she frowned.

It hadn't been a dream, then. She was in the bed. Someone—Luke—must have carried her in and laid her here. So where had *he* slept?

She knew as soon as the thought entered her mind

that it wouldn't have been on the chairs. Luke had needed his sleep as much as she had, and his six-foot length would have been even more uncomfortable than she had been. In any case, he wasn't the type to give in that far. . . .

Slowly she turned her head. The hump of the duvet beside her told her the answer. Like it or not, she and Luke had shared the bed right through the night. And, just at present, with the delicious warmth and comfort still surrounding her, she really didn't feel like objecting.

Hardly knowing what she did, Flair shifted a little nearer to Luke. She could feel the warmth of his body and she sighed and wriggled sensuously, letting all her barriers go for this stolen moment that might have to last her the rest of her life. It was, she thought, like daring the lair of a dangerous animal— a grizzly bear, for instance, or the tiger she had first likened him to. The sense of delight was heightened by the danger. Just for once, with Luke asleep and unconscious of what was happening, she could allow herself the luxury of pleasure in his nearness. The moment he woke she would be away like a frightened bird.

For a little while she lay there, still in the pleasant haze of early waking. Luke's soft, steady breathing was like a whisper in the room. Outside, the world was coming to life; the chattering Twenty-Eights had been joined by a crowd of kookaburras, roaring with laughter at their own dubious jokes. There was the warbling of nesting magpies too, together with other voices Flair couldn't identify.

Her mind was drifting pleasantly when Luke gave

a sudden grunt, rolled over and, before she could move, trapped her in his arms.

Flair lay rigid as two pieces of knowledge forced their way into her mind. One was that Luke was still asleep. The other was that neither of them seemed to have much on in the way of clothes.

With an effort, she controlled her panic. Last night she had been wearing jeans and a shirt, with just a pair of brief panties underneath and no bra because of the heat. Now, she seemed to have just the shirt and panties. So someone had stripped off her jeans, and there were no prizes for guessing who.

Luke himself, as she could tell from the pressure of his warm body against hers, was wearing only a pair of briefs.

Flair closed her eyes and groaned silently. Why, *why* hadn't she got out while the going was good? Why hadn't she slipped out of bed the moment she woke? How on earth had she come to give way to that inexplicable impulse to stay there, even moving closer to him, luxuriating in the comfort of the bed, relishing the dangerous excitement of sharing it with Luke Seager? What had got into her—had she taken leave of her senses?

There was no chance of getting out without waking him. She could only hope that, just as he had turned towards her in his sleep, so he would turn away. And, meanwhile, try not to wake him with her own quickened breathing and wildly-beating heart.

Luke stirred again and his hands moved on her body. Despite herself, Flair's lips parted and a faint moan escaped her as his fingers slid up under her shirt and just touched her breasts. She felt the fingers tighten on her then and gasped as Luke, still apparently half asleep, drew her closer and claimed her mouth with his own. Flair felt the warmth and the length of him, felt him come slowly to awareness, became disturbingly conscious of the hardness of his masculinity throbbing against her. Her thoughts whirled as her surroundings faded, leaving only a world that was solely composed of two bodies that were merging—that must merge—into one. A world of warmth and desire, where nothing else mattered; where hands and fingers and mouths went where they would and were received with delight and welcomed. A world of increasing urgency, where solid flesh and bone seemed to melt, to become fluid with the fire of their passion. A world she had never dreamed existed; had rejected without understanding its full meaning.

A strange lethargy invaded her limbs as she turned in his arms, pressing her body close against his, letting her legs tangle with the hard muscles of his thighs. Her mouth parted under his kiss and she let her mouth move freely with his, exploring, tantalising. She felt his mouth leave hers and turned her head to follow his lips, only to gasp with delight as his tongue flicked into her ear and his teeth bit gently at the lobe. Muttering something she couldn't catch, he burned a fiery trail of kisses down her neck to the fastening of her shirt and nuzzled open the top button to fasten hungrily on the hardened nipples that seemed almost to spring towards him as Flair whimpered and moved sensuously against him.

'Luke . . .' she breathed against his hair. 'Luke. . . .'

Slowly then he withdrew from her, raising himself on his elbow to look down into her face. She saw that his eyes, still shadowed with sleep, were serious, his face grave, and she reached up trembling fingers to stroke the lines from his cheek. He caught at her hand and held it against him, turning to kiss the palm.

'Flair,' he said, and his voice was husky, 'before we go any farther we've got to get one thing clear. I've got to be sure that you know what you're doing—that there'll be no regrets, no recriminations.' He touched her cheek and ran his fingers burningly down the column of her throat to the neck of her shirt, undoing the remaining buttons as he went. 'I've never yet had an unwilling partner. I don't want to start now.' His eyes went to her breasts, swelling towards him, and he groaned and buried his face against them.

Convulsively, Flair gripped him to her. But already her mind was beginning to work again. The moment's respite had told her just where she stood with Luke Seager. It was to be an affair, nothing more. And she knew now, with the shock of an explosion, that she wanted more—much, much more. The feelings that surged through her body whenever Luke touched her weren't just lust and desire. It wasn't merely a streak of unsuspected sensuality that tore at her body. It was more than that. It was love.

As Luke twined his limbs about hers, she knew that much as she longed to be his, she must never let it happen. Because once it had, she would be firmly committed to him for the rest of her life. Branded as his. Now—while that irrevocable step hadn't yet been taken—there was still chance of escape.

Nobody would ever know—least of all Luke—how Flair longed to stay where she was in his arms, responding to his lovemaking with all the fire and passion that surged so tumultuously within her. Nobody would ever know the supreme effort it needed to pull herself away, roll out of his surprised arms and grab her jeans from the floor where they had been left the night before.

'You gave me the option,' she panted as he stared up at her. 'You said you didn't want an unwilling partner. . . .' Clutching the jeans against her, she backed towards the shower-room, flinching under the sudden blaze of anger and frustration in his eyes.

'Damn you!' he ground out. 'You *weren't* unwilling—you wanted it as much as I did. Do you know what they call women like you?' he demanded savagely as she retreated. 'Do you know? And do you know what happens when you try it too often? Just once too often . . . that's all it takes. But it's the man who gets the blame, poor bastard.'

Flair slammed the door, losing the rest of his words as she turned on the shower. Shaking, she cowered under it, terrified that Luke would smash down the door to get at her. If he did that, there would be no hope. Even if he didn't—how were they to get through the rest of the day together? And . . . her body shuddered . . . the night. . . .

There was one thing clear. She couldn't, she *couldn't* go on working for him now. The whole situation had got completely out of hand. Obviously he

had set his sights on an affair with her, whatever her
reactions. And, unfortunately, he was all too well
aware of her physical response to him. What he
didn't know—and must never know—was that
somehow, without ever meaning to, she had fallen in
love with him. That she just had to keep to herself.

For her own sake, she knew she must get away.
There would be nothing but pain now in working
for Luke Seager; seeing him every day, talking to
him, knowing that her love was returned only by a
passing desire. Knowing that one day she was all too
likely to give in, from her own urgent need; and
regret it for the rest of her days.

At last she had to admit that she could stay under
the shower no longer. Slowly she dried herself,
dressed again in the same clothes she had worn yesterday, including the crumpled shirt that had been
her night attire, and stepped warily out.

There was no sign of Luke. And when she looked
into the other rooms they were as empty as the bedroom. Only a note, propped against the kettle, gave
any hint that he had been there.

Flair picked it up and read it. *When you're ready*, it
said, *come over to the gymnasium. I want to finish work
today.*

It wasn't signed.

There was nothing Flair could do but obey. She
ate a hasty breakfast, slipped into a clean white shirt
and made her way to the gymnasium. The prospect
of working all day beside Luke in the enforced inti-
macy of the deserted island was one she would rather
not have faced. But until the job was completed,
there was no other option.

Luke greeted her brusquely, hardly glancing up from what he was doing, and handed her several sheets of paper with the request to carry out some measuring on her own and to consider the decor for the sauna and rest rooms. That would keep them adequately apart for the rest of the morning, Flair reflected as she left him, and strangely she didn't know whether to be glad or sorry. To be with Luke was a sweet pain, a torment she had never before experienced. Yet, now that she knew she loved him, it seemed better than the gnawing ache of being apart from him. An ache, she realised as she began her work in the sauna, that looked like accompanying her through the rest of her life.

It was at about eleven o'clock, just as she began to think about coffee, that she heard the engine.

Straightening, she went over to the window that looked down on the bay and back to the coast. A white motor launch was throbbing its way across the blue water, its wake bubbling and foaming behind it as it came. To her astonishment, she saw that it was making for Blue Island. And beside the blue-clad helmsman was a figure in dazzling yellow.

A moment later Flair knew who it must be, and her heart sank. She watched dully as Luke emerged from the gymnasium and stared out across the bay. Then he too must have recognised the yellow figure, for he gave a shout and set off at a run towards the little harbour.

So Roxanne had grown tired of waiting for him to come back. She had come to see for herself just what was happening on Blue Island.

Flair returned with a sigh to her task. I bet he

won't tell her, she thought with a twist of bitter humour. Though Roxanne's sharp enough to guess quite a lot. It might be quite interesting to see her reaction.

By the time Flair arrived at the chalet to make coffee, the boat had moored against Luke's launch in the harbour, and as Flair turned up the winding path through the trees she could see Luke holding out his hand to Roxanne, to help her ashore. The American girl certainly knew how to take advantage of every situation—the moment her foot touched land she was in Luke's arms, though whether by her design or his Flair couldn't tell. She turned abruptly away and went into the chalet.

The other two arrived just as coffee was ready. Flair put three cups on the tray with the coffee-pot and carried it out to the verandah.

'My, this is service!' Roxanne exclaimed gaily. 'You certainly know how to take care of yourself, Luke. He loves his creature comforts, Miss Pattison, or maybe you've noticed that already?'

Her dark eyes were sparkling with malice as she looked at Flair, who shrugged as she put the tray down on a low table.

'I'm afraid I've been too busy to notice much,' she answered casually. 'Blue Island's going to be marvellous for holidays when it's finished, but just at present it spells work, and hard work at that.' She let her eyes drift over the other girl's expensive-looking yellow jumpsuit, filled to perfection by the voluptuous curves beneath. 'It'll be nice to have another pair of hands.'

Roxanne gave a yelp of laughter. 'Honey, I

haven't come here to *work*! Well, not unless you
count being a messenger work, and even *I* can't do
that—not when it means a boat trip on a lovely
morning to the most attractive man I know.' She
turned to Luke and reached up to let her slender
fingers wander through the hair at the back of his
neck. 'How about you, Luke baby? Do you think
I've earned a reward?'

'Could be,' he answered noncommittally.
'Depends what sort of reward you have in mind.'

Roxanne laughed again, this time a deep-throated
gurgle. 'Well, I don't really think *that* needs much
explaining, do you?' she murmured suggestively.
'And it's a reward you might even enjoy giving
me. . . .'

Flair stood up abruptly and gathered up her cup.
They'd be making love under her very eyes in a
moment! She turned to go back into the chalet, but
Luke's voice arrested her.

'Flair, don't go.' Half turning, she could see his
fingers playing with Roxanne's mass of dark hair.
'Look, I've had an idea. You've been working pretty
hard out here, and I reckon you've had just about
enough. Why don't you go on back with Roxanne's
boat? I can finish what needs to be done on my own,
and Roxanne can have a look around the island and
come on back with me later, how'd that be?'

Stunned, Flair turned and stared down at him.
He was lying back in a sunlounger, perfectly at ease
and vitally masculine in his shorts that displayed
tanned, muscular legs, and his shirt unbuttoned
almost to the waist. Blue eyes glinted up at her and
strong white teeth flashed as he smiled a slow, lazy

smile that turned her heart over.

He wanted to get rid of her, and it didn't take a genius to work out why. She risked a quick glance at Roxanne and saw triumph on the sultry face. Just how much work would get done once she was out of the way? she wondered bitterly. Luke had been a hard taskmaster during the past two days—would he be so dedicated with Roxanne around? It didn't seem very likely.

Flair knew a quick blaze of jealousy. She stamped it down ruthlessly. She'd had her chance—her flesh tingled again as she remembered those moments in the bed this morning—and she'd rejected it. And she'd been *right*, she told herself fiercely. Even if Roxanne could be magically whisked away, leaving Flair and Luke alone again, things wouldn't— couldn't—be any different. This was the best thing that could happen. The *only* thing.

Luke was still watching her, an enigmatic expression in his eyes.

'Well?' he asked softly. 'Don't you think that's a good idea?'

'Yes, of course,' Flair said quietly, hoping that the misery in her heart wasn't sounding in her voice. 'It's a very good idea. I—I'll just collect my things. Your boatman won't want to hang around too long.'

She didn't miss the flash of pleasure in the American girl's eyes as she turned back to the chalet. But it was nothing to do with her, she reminded herself, hastily packing the bag she'd brought with her. She couldn't have Luke herself—not the way she wanted him. And she didn't have any right to prevent anyone else from enjoying what he had to give.

So why, she wondered as the boat left the tiny harbour and sped away from Blue Island—why did she feel like a naughty girl who'd been sent home early from a party? Why was her unhappiness a weight so heavy that she was surprised it didn't sink the boat?

Was she never to be free of Lucifer's brand?

CHAPTER FIVE

ONCE back in Perth, Flair went straight home. She felt tired, scruffy and dishevelled, needing a good long shower and completely fresh change of clothes. The short time she had spent on Blue Island seemed an age. She felt that she wouldn't be surprised to see herself looking ten years older.

The house was empty, and Flair felt herself begin to relax under the shower. She let the water flow over her body, sponging herself with shower gel, revelling in the clean, sharp smell of it. It was her second long shower of the day, yet she felt the need for thorough cleansing; something to wash away the memories of the morning, something to give her a fresh start. Shame washed over her with the water as she remembered her sensual response to Luke's advances, the surge of delight she had experienced as his hands explored her body and his mouth trailed kisses like flames from her eyelids to her breasts. No wonder he had been angry at her final rejection. No wonder he had left her, sent her back to the mainland and kept Roxanne, so much more compliant, with him. Just what would happen during the afternoon, on those white beaches? Flair mused bitterly as she washed her hair until it squeaked. But there was really no need to wonder. She could guess.

Leaving the shower at last, and slipping on a long

white robe of broderie anglaise, she wandered into
the sitting-room and stopped in surprise to see her
father there, stretched out in his favourite armchair
with his eyes closed.

She crossed over the room and was looking down
at him with some anxiety when he opened his eyes
and smiled at her, his thin face creased with affection.

'I didn't hear you come in,' Flair said. 'Is anything the matter? You look exhausted.'

'Nothing's the matter, my dear.' Jeff eased himself
upright in the chair and ran his fingers through his
faded coppery hair. 'I've just been working rather
hard these past few days on the designs for the new
motel. You're back sooner than I expected. Did
everything go well?'

Flair turned away. How could she tell him what
had really happened? It was bad enough having to
tell him that she wasn't going to continue working
for Luke—and she hadn't even decided how she was
going to explain *that*. She turned back and gave her
father a brilliant smile.

'Yes, fine. We got most of the job finished by this
morning. Luke's still over there, tying up some loose
ends.'

'*Luke* is?' Jeff frowned. 'How did you get back,
then?'

'Oh, Roxanne turned up this morning—with a
message, I think she said,' Flair answered carelessly.
'Luke suggested I take the chance to come back early
in her boat and she stayed on to look round. She
hadn't been there before.'

'*Roxanne* arrived? With a message, you say? Hmm.'

Jeff looked thoughtful. 'Wonder what that was about.'

'Oh, it was probably just an excuse,' Flair remarked, as if the subject didn't interest her. 'She does seem on rather friendly terms with Luke, after all.'

Jeff shot her a glance. 'Does she? Well, that may be, but any message she's likely to take him could still be interesting. Did she say if it was from her father?'

'Her father? No, why should it be?'

'Why should——' Jeff broke off and laughed. 'Don't tell me you don't know who Roxanne is? Who her father is?'

Flair flung herself into an armchair and stared at him. 'No, I don't. Why? Are they important? All I know is Roxanne's American, and I presume her father is too.'

'He certainly is. Well, you haven't been here long, I know, but I'm rather surprised that Luke hasn't put you in the picture. Maybe things aren't so far advanced as I'd thought.'

'Dad,' Flair said patiently, 'if we're going to talk in riddles give me fair warning so I can think up a few. *What* picture? *What* things? Just who are Roxanne and her daddy? And what do they have to do with Luke, apart from the obvious?'

Jeff smiled at her, unperturbed by her exasperation.

'You know, there are times when you're very like your mother,' he observed. 'In the nicest possible way, of course. I wonder how she's getting on without you. . . . All right, all right!' He held up both hands to ward off the cushion Flair was aiming at him. 'I'll come clean. Well, Roxanne is the daughter—the only child, in fact—of Hailey Ryan. Have you heard of *him*?'

'*Hailey* Ryan?' Flair repeated. 'You mean Hailey Ryan of Ryan Hotels? The big American chain— they've just opened one in London and another in Paris? You mean *he's* Roxanne's father?'

'That's right. Now do you see why I'm interested? The talk is that Ryan and Seager are considering a merger, at least in this country. It could be a big thing for Luke if it goes through and it won't do Ryan much harm, either. He hasn't been able to get so much as a toe in Australia so far, and it's Luke who can let him in if he wants.'

'But would he want? I mean, he'd be giving up a lot of what he's built up.'

'No, not really. The name would stick, I think, and Luke would still be kingpin here. It would help him to expand more, though, and of course he'd have a finger in the Ryan pie worldwide. I told you, it could mean a really big thing for him.'

'And you think Roxanne came over this morning with some message from her father to do with this?'

Jeff shrugged. 'Could be. Can you think of any other reason?'

Flair could, and especially for Roxanne's staying behind on the island while she herself was sent home like a schoolgirl. She said nothing, however, and thought over the new situation.

Obviously Roxanne was aware of her father's interest in Luke—or rather, in Seager Hotels. It was Roxanne's own interest that was in Luke himself.

And clearly, if Luke, already doing well with his own hotel chain, were also to go in with Hailey Ryan, he would be a good catch for someone like Roxanne. Flair recalled the American girl's words at their first meeting—the sneer about Flair looking for a wealthy hotelier. The idea had been the first to come to her mind just because it was her own plan.

As for Luke, Roxanne would be the ideal match. It would clinch the merger to find Roxanne only too ready to throw herself at him. Not only a Ryan-Seager Hotel merger, but marriage with the heiress to all the Ryan share—that couldn't be bad!

Flair glanced up to find her father watching her quizzically. She blushed and rose quickly to her feet. He mustn't see that it mattered to her.

'I'm parched,' she said, making for the kitchen. 'Want a drink, Dad? Something long and icy?'

'Fine.' He waited until she returned with a drink and, taking his and thanking her, added: 'You are happy here, aren't you, Flair? I mean, with me and the country, and your job. You are getting along all right?'

'Yes, of course,' she answered automatically, then bit her lip. Somehow she had to tell him she was leaving Luke, and what assumption was he going to make then?

She glanced at her father and was struck afresh by his tiredness. Perhaps this talk of a merger was worrying him more than he revealed. After all, it would probably mean a good deal to him too. There would be a lot more work if Luke were to expand even more than he was already doing—but would the work come to Jeff Pattison or to some American architect brought in by Hailey Ryan? Was that what was in his mind?

'I'm glad you're happy,' Jeff said quietly. 'I was afraid—when I wrote asking you to come out—that you wouldn't like it. You wouldn't have stayed long in that case—and I admit I'm very selfish and want you to stay as long as possible. I've missed you a great deal over these past years, Flair. One keeps in touch, but it isn't the same. The little, everyday things—they can never be replaced.'

Flair reached over and took his hand, her eyes brimming. She knew exactly what he meant. There'd been so many times when she had needed him too. Coming home from school; weekend outings. The times when her bicycle had had a puncture, or her skipping-rope had needed its handles mending. The times when she'd watched other girls at the boarding school being fetched by their fathers. Her father had known about those things and missed them too.

'I'm sorry, Flair,' said Jeff, and she squeezed his hand, the moment of self-pity gone.

'It wasn't your fault, Dad. It wasn't anyone's fault really.'

'I wanted your mother to come, you know,' he told her. 'But I knew she wouldn't It was the old story of the irresistible force and the immovable object. I had to come; she had to stay.'

'I know. It's all right.'

'Yes, it's all right now,' he said, smiling at her. 'You're here and you've got your job—it's a good job, Flair, and Luke's a fine man. I've got a lot of reason to be grateful to him. It's meant a lot to me to see you getting on so well.'

'I'm glad,' she said weakly, and knew that it was impossible to tell Jeff now that she wasn't working for Luke any more. Not so soon, anyway. Maybe later, when she had had time to look around—maybe then she could find something else, tell Jeff that she wanted to widen her experience. There had to be some way out—but she knew that she couldn't take it now. Not until Jeff had got used to having a daughter again. Not until the talk of the merger was less uncertain.

They sat for a long time, talking of Flair's childhood and of their lives since Jeff had come to Australia, and when they finally decided it was time for a meal Flair felt that she knew her father better than she had ever done before. Better even than she knew her mother, she reflected as she dressed for their meal out, Jeff having decided that this evening was to be a special one. Susan had always been cool in her attitude to personal relationships—maybe that was why the marriage had broken up with so little acrimony. It had never meant all that much to her to begin with. And even towards Flair, her mother had always maintained a reserve it was impossible to penetrate. It wasn't done deliberately—Flair had long realised that—it was just her nature. She was an exceptionally private kind of person, and liked to keep it that way.

Whereas Jeff was slowly revealing a warmth of nature that surprised his daughter. She wondered just what her parents' marriage had been like in its private moments. Had Jeff been a passionate man, an ardent lover? And she herself—whom did she take after? Susan, with her cool reserve—or Jeff, with what she was beginning to realise was a deeply loving personality?

Luke's face came into her mind and she recalled those moments only this morning when they had lain together in the bed and desire had surged within her, almost impossible to control. Heat flooded her body at the memory. She had never felt that reaction to any man before, had thought herself as cool as her mother and been thankful for it. Now she wished that she had never discovered the truth about herself—the truth that she loved Luke, deeply and irrevocably, that she yearned for his touch, his kiss, his caress. And that she had to repress her yearning; never let him or anyone else know of it. Had to carry it with her, unfulfilled, for ever.

Jeff took her to a restaurant on the edge of King's Park for dinner. They sat in a wide window, gazing out over Perth at the darkness aglow with the coloured lights of the city, split by the black sweep of the Swan river with the streak of the Narrows Bridge just below them. Beyond the town rose the darker humps of the Darling Ranges, and Flair could see the lights of an aircraft approaching the airport. It was only a short time since she herself had been circling up there, gazing down with excitement and anticipation at these very same lights. It seemed half a lifetime ago.

The meal was delicious. Somehow Flair had forgotten lunch, and she now found herself ravenously hungry. Studying the extensive menu, she finally decided on watermelon, followed by dhufish which was accompanied by a piquant fruit salad, and

finished with that most Australian of desserts, pav-
lova—an unbelievably high concoction of pink
merinque filled with strawberries and cream.
Satisfied at last, she laid down her spoon and smiled
at her father.

'That was superb,' she thanked him. 'And it's such
a marvellous place. Thank you for bringing me.'

'It's a delight to be able to,' he told her sincerely.
'Now, what about some coffee and a liqueur to round
it off? And then——' His eyes, glancing over Flair's
shoulder towards the door, widened with some
surprise. 'Well, look who's here!'

She didn't need to ask. It could be only one
person—the man who was never completely out of
her thoughts, who filled her mind more than she
liked. The man who had in a few short weeks turned
upside down her ambitions, her principles, her whole
attitude to life, leaving her gasping like a fish on
shore.

Slowly, reluctantly, she turned her head and
watched with a resigned apathy as Luke entered the
restaurant. He looked suavely handsome tonight, she
registered, in his dark brown suit that set off the
burning gold of his hair and tanned face. Gold cuff-
links flashed from his strong wrists and the broad
band of his Rolex wristwatch gleamed. Everything
about him spelled success—including the woman
who stood with him as they waited to be led to their
table.

And, of course, that had to be Roxanne, looking
more beautiful than ever in a gold sheath of a dress
that accentuated every line of her sumptuous figure.
The dark hair swirled around her shoulders and

sultry brown eyes smouldered between long thick lashes. Her dress was cut daringly low at the front; at the back it dipped almost to waist level.

Jeff was smiling, raising his hand to attract attention. If it had been left to Flair she would have made no sign, merely hoped that Luke's table was out of sight of their own; after the events of the morning, she would have liked never to have to face Luke again. But she summoned up a smile as her employer caught sight of them and drew Roxanne after him across the restaurant.

'So you made it back all right,' he greeted Flair casually. 'Hi, Jeff, how's it going?'

'Good,' Jeff answered in the Australian idiom. 'Evening, Miss Ryan. How did you like Blue Island?'

'Oh, just beautiful,' the American girl exclaimed. 'Especially the bathing beaches,' she added with a sideways glance at Flair. 'Luke and I spent the whole afternoon on one, a real gem. It was great, wasn't it, honey? We just didn't know how to tear ourselves away.'

'Still, you managed it,' Flair commented. 'And I'm sure you must have been a great help to Luke.'

'She was indeed,' Luke agreed dryly. 'Gave me a good idea of some of the ways my guests will enjoy themselves.'

Flair felt her cheeks flame, and bent her head. She stirred her coffee and began to sip it, trying not to listen to the conversation that was going on around her.

'. . . have a long talk with you some time,' Jeff was saying, and she glanced up, aware of a serious note in his voice. So he *was* worrying about the merger. Luke was looking thoughtful.

'Mmm. Have to be tomorrow, then, if it's urgent. I want to head down towards Albany the day after.' His eyes turned to Flair and she steeled herself to meet their compelling blue without betraying her feelings. 'Hope you haven't unpacked too much— it'll be another early start, I'm afraid. We'll have to get through as much as we can in the office tomorrow.'

Flair nodded. Misery lay in her stomach like a lead weight. He didn't even know she cared! Well, it was the way she wanted it—but oh, to see some answering light in those cold blue eyes. And they were going on another trip together, another series of days and nights, in close contact yet without any real communication between them. If only she could hand him her notice—but a glance at her father, an understanding of the pride and delight he was taking in this meeting, told her she couldn't. She had to go through with it.

Roxanne, too, was looking peeved. She pouted and fluttered her lashes at Luke as she said: 'But honey, you've only just come back. You're as bad as Pop—you hotel men are always the same, always *busy*.'

Luke smiled down at her. 'It's the way we make our living, Roxy. And you must admit you like *that*. Anyway, our table's ready now. We'll say cheerio, then,' he added to Jeff. 'I'll make time for that talk.' And, with a curt nod to Flair, 'Be as early as you can in the office tomorrow, will you? There's a hell of a lot of work to get through.'

Through a mist of tears, Flair watched them walk away to their table. This was the way it was going to be—always, she told herself. She was just going to have to start getting used to it.

She was at the hotel early next morning and hard at work when Luke arrived. He said little to her, beyond what was necessary, and after asking whether her father would still be at home, went out again. He did not return until after lunch.

Flair wanted to ask what he and Jeff had discussed, but knew Luke wouldn't tell her. No doubt Jeff would that evening, but she found it hard to wait, wondering uneasily whether Luke's stern face and tight lips had anything to do with it. Whatever the subject had been, it didn't seem to have pleased him.

But when she reached home, Jeff wasn't there. He'd left a note saying he'd had to go off urgently on another job and wouldn't be back until late. As she had an early start to make next day, better not wait up for him. He'd see her when she got back.

So Flair had to go to bed still wondering; and the questions were still unanswered in her mind as she rose next morning, ate her breakfast and was ready for Luke when he called for her in the grey light of early morning.

Neither of them spoke much during the early part of the drive. Once out of Perth the road was straight and long. Flair sat quietly in the car, looking out at the beauty of the bush; the flowers that carpeted the ground and climbed and sprawled over many of the shrubs and trees; the brilliant colours of parrots and other birds flying across in front of the car. When they stopped for a flask of coffee, she could hear their strident calls and whistles; a few miles on, when they came suddenly on a family of kangaroos bounding along the road, she gave a cry of excitement, and couldn't repress her laughter as the strange animals panicked, hopping first one way, then the other, the baby 'joey' colliding with its mother in its eagerness to scramble into her pouch. The mother used her front paws to help it in, and Flair choked with giggles as she saw first a hind leg, then an ear poke out as the joey twisted and turned inside the furry pouch.

'It's almost too big to go in at all,' Luke remarked, just as amused. 'Real vacuum-packing, that is. But it won't survive much longer if mum and dad don't teach it better road drill.'

'Do many get killed on the roads?' Flair asked, thinking of sheep and ponies in some of the wilder parts of England. Luke nodded.

'Quite a fair number. People who drive a lot on bush roads have roo-bars fitted to their cars—you must have seen them. Otherwise they'll do a lot of damage. The worst is when the mother gets killed and the joey survives.'

'Can't they be saved?' Flair asked, and Luke shrugged.

'Depends if they're found, and who by. People take 'em to the wildlife parks—there's one just out of Perth, and the big one up at Yanchep. I've seen quite little joeys there, all curled up in old woolly pullovers—can't thrive unless they're in a bag, you see—and feeding out of babies' bottles. Of course, in big farming country they're a pest. People shoot them.'

'Oh no! Such lovely animals,' Flair said in distress.

'Depends whether they're taking your living away,' Luke told her. 'And there doesn't seem to be much risk of them becoming extinct.'

They drove on, silent again, but this time the quality of silence was different. The strain had gone out of it. It was almost—companionable, Flair thought, the word surprising her. Would she have thought, only twenty-four hours ago, that she could ever feel *companionable* with Luke Seager?

'We're heading down the Leeuwin Way,' Luke said suddenly, breaking the silence. 'Keeps pretty well along the coast—there's some nice places along it. Thought it'd give you a bit more view of Australia.'

'Thank you,' said Flair, surprised. She had assumed Luke was in a hurry to get to his motel site, too much of a hurry to bother about showing her any of the beauty spots along the way. She glanced about her with renewed appreciation. 'Whereabouts are we now? And why is it called the Leeuwin Way?'

He indicated the glove compartment. 'Maps and booklets in there, if you want to follow the route. We're coming into Mandurah now. And Leeuwin comes from a lighthouse at Cape Leeuwin. It was called after a Dutch ship—the one that did the original survey of the area. Means Lioness, or so they told me at school.'

Flair sat back in her seat, glancing at the maps

every so often, but mostly too enthralled with the beautiful country they were passing through. To either side rose tall eucalyptus trees; later, Luke told her, they would be in big tree country, among the karri and jarrah forests, and farther on among the giant tingle trees, so huge that you could drive an estate wagon into their hollowed-out trunks. 'And most of them are hollow,' he added. 'Burnt and blackened by centuries of lightning storms and bush fires. But they seem to survive it all.'

The bush was thickly covered at ground level by the rainbow colours of the wildflowers—like some huge exotic garden gone mad, Flair thought. Among the maps she had found a booklet describing some of the wildflowers and she flipped through the pages, trying to imprint on her mind the pictures of leschenaultia, as blue as Luke's eyes, kangaroo paw with its strange formation, and the bright yellow cones of the banksia. Other names were more familiar to her and she found it easy to recognise some of the varieties of clematis, myrtles, orchids and hibiscus, but the vast majority of the flowers she saw were strange and she could only gasp at their apparently infinite variety and beauty.

The journey, interspersed with lunch at the seaside town of Bunbury and a further stop at Busselton, with its mile-long jetty stretching out into the Indian Ocean, was one of the happiest that Flair had ever known. For once—probably because they kept off any personal issues, assuming the roles of visitor and guide—she and Luke were in complete accord. Flair felt her love grow almost tangibly deeper and stronger in this milder climate. Yet Luke, still wearing an air of reserve and aloofness with his friendliness, seemed totally unaware of her feelings. And because of this Flair's happiness had a bitter-sweet tinge to it. If only things could have been different, she mused as they strolled along the white beach at Busselton. And she was suddenly shaken by a rush of desire stronger than any she had yet known. Only a tremendous effort of self-control kept her from his arms at that moment. She wanted to fling herself at him, hold him closely, sob out her love . . . but it was useless. He wouldn't understand. He would take what she had to give—oh yes, she thought bitterly, Luke Seager wasn't a man to pass up an opportunity—and then he would pass on, never knowing just what she had given him. Never knowing that he had left her with nothing.

She couldn't risk it. And, suddenly afraid of the tears that threatened, she turned away and began to walk back to the car.

Afterwards, the journey was a kaleidoscope to Flair. She recalled Peppermint Bay, Cosy Corner—which was anything but cosy, with the breakers of the Indian Ocean hurling themselves in a spray of white foam against the savage rocks and cliffs—Hamelin Bay and Cape Naturaliste; the broad main street of Margaret River and the signs encouraging visits to the Jewel, Lake and Mammoth Caves—visits, Luke said, that would have to wait for another day. Tonight they were aiming to stay at Augusta and time was running on.

Flair had been half dreading, half longing for the night. Sitting beside Luke in the car all day, her shoulder occasionally brushing his, sharing with him the experience of the drive south, her instincts had been so aroused that she felt that there was no other course open to her but to give in. Perhaps if she did, she would then be free of him . . . perhaps the brand was washed out when frustration was satisfied. . . . In her heart, she knew it couldn't be true; that once possessed by Luke she would be irreversibly his. But her longing had grown to such a pitch that she almost believed it, almost thought it worth the risk.

They arrived at last in a small, unpretentious sea-side settlement near Augusta and drew up in front of a motel, its buildings clearly in need of a coat of paint. The main building comprised the reception office and a restaurant, and Luke came round and opened Flair's door, indicating that she should accompany him inside.

Nervous now, and not at all sure of herself, she followed him, finding herself in a shabby but pleasantly-furnished office, with comfortable seats and faded decorations. It was spotlessly clean, but to Flair's eyes there were immediately discrepancies, things that could and should have been put right. She was surprised that the fastidious Luke should consider staying here, and wondered if it might be that he was unlikely to meet anyone he knew.

But that thought was quickly dismissed as an elderly man came through a door at the back and stared at them. There was a moment's surprised silence, then his nut-brown face split into a wide grin and he came quickly forward and slapped Luke on the back.

'Luke, me old mate, it's good to see you! How're you going? My word, it's a long time since you've

been down this way. Wait a mo, while I call Lance.'
He turned and bellowed into the back regions. 'Hey,
Lance, come and look who's here. It's Luke—Luke
Seager, doing a bit of slumming!' He glanced at Flair
and said mischievously, 'There wouldn't be any—
er—*ulterior motive* for this visit, would there now?'

'No such thing, you evil-minded old ocker,' Luke
said cheerfully. 'We want two rooms for the night—
two, you get that? And one of those meals you're so
good at knocking up out of nothing, because knowing
you there won't be a thing worth eating in the
pantry!'

'Insults, that's all I ever get from this bloke,' the
little man told Flair plaintively. 'Nothing but slander
and insults. Now, this is me boy, and I tell you this,
if you're looking for a man you don't need to look
no further. Forget him——' he waved an expressive
hand at Luke '—and take a look at this.'

Flair, smiling, did as she was told. The newcomer
gave his father an exasperated half-grin which
widened as he saw Luke and greeted him. Then he
turned to Flair, and she saw his eyes darken with
admiration.

'Hul*lo*.' He held out his hand and Flair took it,
liking the firm handshake he gave her and looking
at him with interest. Tall, on the rangy side, with
brown curls and a merry face, he would grow very
like his gnome-like father as he aged, but just now,
only a couple of years older than she was herself, he
had an air of easy friendliness that was instantly
attractive.

'Take no notice of Dad,' he said in a pleasant
voice. 'He just likes to jabber, Miss——'

'Flair Pattison,' Luke said quickly. 'And this is Lance Carnagy, and his disreputable old father Dougie. You needn't take any notice of either of them, actually, Lance is only polite for the first half-hour!'

'Good to know you, Flair,' said Dougie, offering her a horny hand. 'But tell me, what's a nice girl like you doing travelling around with a guy like Luke here?'

'She's my personal assistant, and I don't want any cracks about that either,' Luke told him. 'We're on our way down to see the Albany site and I thought I'd let her see what hotels were like in Australia before I came on the scene.'

'Huh, very funny,' the old man grunted. 'He thinks we're a real slum here,' he confided to Flair. 'But I tell him, that's the way we are and it's the way people seem to like us. Folk don't have to stand on ceremony when they come here for a bit of rest. Crabbing, fishing, bit of beachcombing—that's what our guests like to do, and they don't want nothing posh for that, just a comfortable bed and some good tucker. And that's what we give 'em. I'll admit we don't make a fortune—not like old Luke here—but what'd we do with it if we did? We don't want to live no other way.'

'All right, cut the sob-story,' Luke remarked. 'We've had a long drive and we're ready for a meal as soon as you can get it together. Which rooms are you putting us in?'

'Let's see now,' Lance consulted a chart. 'Couple at the end of the row suit you?' He handed Luke the keys. 'See you a bit later in the restaurant, then.' He smiled at Flair, showing even white teeth. 'Hope you'll be comfortable, Flair—if there's anything you want, just come along and ask. See you later—we'll have a talk then, maybe.'

'They're a great couple, Dougie and Lance,' Luke observed, leading the way to the end of the row and fitting a key in one of the doors. 'But they'll never make anything of this place. Just haven't got the drive. It's never been any different all the years I've known them, and it never will.'

'But that's how they *like* it,' Flair said indignantly. 'And so do I—it's got an atmosphere all its own. And the people come here for that, I'm sure, just like Dougie said.'

'Well, of course,' said Luke, looking faintly amused. 'I never said anything else, did I?' And he stood back for Flair to go into the room. 'Here's your key. I'll be next door if you want anything. Dinner in about an hour, shall we say?' And before Flair could speak, he had bowed himself gravely out of the room and closed the door.

Flair stood quite still. She wasn't sure what she had expected—after all, Luke hadn't put foot or finger wrong all day, had been an ideal companion. But now, alone after what must have been a pleasant day for him too—she just hadn't expected him to leave her quite so abruptly.

Of course, he wouldn't stay too long because of Dougie and Lance—though surely if they knew Luke well they knew his reputation with women. Perhaps he wanted to go along and talk with them before dinner. In any case, she had to start accepting that he just wasn't interested in her any more. She had rejected him yesterday—it was hardly likely he would risk another snub like that. Especially with Roxanne Ryan only too eager to co-operate. No— as far as Luke Seager was concerned, Flair was nothing more than an employee now. And wasn't that, after all, what she'd wanted from the start?

She was ready when Luke banged on the door an hour later, wearing a soft aquamarine dress with a cowl neck, its clear colour complementing her smooth bronze hair and matching her sea-green eyes. Luke was casually elegant in dark brown shirt and cream slacks, his hair still damp from the shower. He smiled at her but looked abstracted. Chilled, Flair walked silently beside him to the restaurant.

There she discovered that Dougie and Lance were eating with them. The food, she was told, had been cooked by Dougie in honour of their coming, but was being finished by the regular cook. Dougie, she discovered with some surprise, was an accomplished chef and had worked in some quite large hotels.

'Too much for me, though,' he told her as they began on a delicious dish made of local crab. 'Too much rush and fuss. I got out as soon as I could afford this place. I like a quiet life.' He shot a look at Flair and his face crinkled with mischief. 'Mind you, if I thought I could have a personal assistant like you, I might think again about going for the big time, what do you say, Lance?'

'Suits me,' Lance grinned. He'd been gazing at Flair with open admiration ever since their arrival in the restaurant, and Flair gave him a quick smile, liking his cheerful, open face and direct glance.

'Well, any time you've got a job going,' she said,

and Lance took her up quickly.

'Chance 'd be a fine thing! But you can bet we'd let you know straight off.'

And Dougie, looking from one to the other with a sudden shrewdness in his bright gaze, added quietly: 'We just might, at that. We just might.' And then, to Luke: 'You'd better watch the way you treat this sheila, Luke. My boy's got his eye on her already, I can see that.'

There was a sudden, tiny silence. Flair looked quickly up at Lance and saw that he had flushed a deep red. Luke's face was still and emotionless, Dougie's unwontedly serious. With a sudden need to get things back to the joking banter of a few minutes earlier, Flair said brightly: 'Well, I can't come to you yet, I'm afraid—I have to give Luke a month's written notice to leave. And I don't happen to have brought a pen with me!'

The tension eased and the evening continued with a good deal of laughter. But as it grew later, Flair found herself growing increasingly aware of Luke's eyes fixed on her and Lance as they sat, a little apart from the other two, talking quietly.

An awareness that went with her as Lance walked her back to her room, slipping a friendly arm round her shoulders as he did so. And that she felt with some force as he gave her a tentative goodnight kiss and she looked past him to see Luke standing at the restaurant door and gazing into the darkness.

Whether he could actually see them or not, she wasn't sure. But—just in case—she slipped her arms around Lance's neck and responded with an enthusiasm that surprised them both.

CHAPTER SIX

FLAIR breakfasted alone next morning, making coffee and pouring milk over the small pack of cereal provided in the room. She ate by the window, looking out over the small beach where already people were beginning the day's activities, preparing for crabbing or fishing expeditions or just setting up deck chairs. For Australia it was still only spring, though to Flair it was pleasantly warm and summery, but she guessed that with such a climate there were always a few people taking advantage of the beaches.

As she finished breakfast and checked to see that she'd packed everything, she noticed Lance approaching the chalet, tall and brown in clean white shirt and shorts, and went to the door to meet him.

'Good morning—isn't it lovely?' She smiled at him, thinking again what a pleasant young man he was. 'I was just thinking of a walk along the beach— I think there's about half an hour before Luke wants to leave.'

'That was my idea, too,' he answered, and they both laughed, then set off towards the sea, talking easily and naturally like old friends. It was a pity she couldn't fall in love with someone like Lance, Flair thought wistfully. Someone easygoing, kindhearted and unfussy. Life could be very pleasant with such a man.

When they returned, she found Luke already packing their bags into the car. He glanced up and gave her a brief nod before continuing his conversation with Dougie. Her heart sank. Things had been so easy, so friendly yesterday. Now it seemed that they were back to the strained silences and abrasiveness of the day before. And why? Just because she'd talked with Lance—kissed him goodnight—walked with him on the beach? Just why should Luke Seager object to that?

'Now, don't forget, Flair,' said Dougie as she took her leave of him, 'you come back here any time you like. We might not be up to much, but we know how to make people feel welcome, ain't that right, Lance?'

'Too right,' Lance nodded, and he took Flair's hand shyly. 'You come back as soon as you can.'

'I will, I promise.' Flair hesitated, then reached up and gave him a kiss. 'Maybe I'll bring Dad when we have our holiday. It would do him good to be here.'

Luke got into the estate wagon and reached over to open Flair's door. She got in beside him and Lance closed it. The car accelerated smoothly away.

'That was nice,' said Flair after a moment's silence. 'I enjoyed meeting Dougie and Lance.'

'And especially Lance,' Luke commented.

'Well, why not? He's about my own age, he's pleasant and friendly—why shouldn't I enjoy meeting him?' She glanced at Luke and noted the stiff line of his face, the tension in his jaw. 'Why should it bother you, anyway? Do you think I'm going to seduce him?'

'How should I know what you're going to do?' he

demanded savagely. 'You open those big green eyes of yours, flutter your eyelashes a bit and what's a man to do—any man? You're not just dynamite, Flair, you're atomic, or maybe you hadn't realised that. That's what you'd say, anyway—with your sweet-little-innocent act. Your come-on glances and sighs, your teasing and drawing back. I told you, you'll do it once too often.'

'I don't——' Flair began, but he went on as if she hadn't spoken.

'You tried it on me first, thinking you'd be clever and show me I wasn't the Casanova you'd been told I was. Then when things started to get out of hand, you got scared. Now you're doing it to young Lance, thinking he'll be easier game, no doubt. String him along, tease him a bit—a glance here, a kiss there, a bit of handholding and cuddling under the stars. And when you've got him so that he doesn't know what to do, you'll be off, won't you, off and away, with another broken heart to dangle from your belt.'

'*No!*' To her dismay, Flair felt tears spring into her eyes, brimming over before she could stop them. 'No, it's not like that—I've never—you can't think I——'

'Can't I?' Luke answered grimly. Then, with a glance at her tear-streaked face, he added in tones of disgust, 'And that's *all* I need—a whingeing woman. My God, why did I ever bring you on this trip?'

'I can't imagine!' she flung back at him. 'Oh, yesterday was fine—you seemed almost human—but today we're back to normal, aren't we? You know what you are? You're a mixture between a bully, a slavedriver and a—a sex-maniac. In fact, that's what

you are most. It's all you ever think of, when you're
not actually planning how to make more and more
money. It's all you seem to think of when I'm
around, anyway, and I can't see that it's just me.
And you talk about *me* being a tease—what about
you? *You* don't want me—but you don't want anyone
else to have me either. Talk about dog-in-the-
manger!'

Luke drove in silence, his mouth tight, for another
mile. Then he swung the big estate wagon off the
main road and into a dirt road, running between
the great trees that Flair only now fully noticed. Still
shaking with anger and with fear at what might be
going to happen next, she stared in awe at the huge
giants that rose all around them. The tingle trees,
she realised dimly; and at the same time noticed that
the sky had darkened and it was beginning to rain.

The rain was cascading down by the time Luke
stopped the car. It streamed off the trees like a
waterfall, gathering in foaming pools around their
roots. It formed a curtain in front of the windscreen
and lashed at the wide windows. Luke let the car
bump slowly down a track between the great trunks
until they reached a small glade; he steered the
vehicle into the vast hollowed-out bole of the largest
tree Flair had ever seen, and in the comparative
shelter he stopped and turned to her.

She did not wait for more. With a stifled gasp of
pure fear, she wrenched open the door and almost
fell from the car in her desperation to escape. Where
she would go, or how, she had no idea—her one
driving need was to get away—away from this man
who had such a devastating effect on her, whose eyes

burned into hers, whose arms were like iron bands
yet filled her with longing when they held her. His
passion left her weak and trembling; his anger was
something she dreaded to the depths of her soul.

'Flair!' he shouted as she ran off through the dense
foliage that grew between the huge trunks, her head
down against the torrential rain. 'Flair, come back—
you little *fool*——'

The rest of his words were lost as Flair found herself tangled in a web of undergrowth, fighting with
twining green leaves that showered water over her,
drenching her to the skin. Her shirt and jeans clung
to her as she twisted and turned, sobbing frantically
in her now totally irrational terror. It was as if they
were animals, living tentacles that caught and
gripped her, entangling her arms and legs, snaking
round her waist and neck, tightening their hold as
she struggled. They seemed to menace her and,
suddenly frighteningly aware of the alien nature of
this strange forest with its monster trees and sinister,
huge-leaved plants, she began to scream.

'*Flair!* Stop panicking, for God's sake, and let me
get you free of that lot!' Gently, Luke held and dis-
entangled her, unwinding the clinging stems from
her limbs and setting her carefully back on the path.
'There, you silly little owl . . .' He caught her to him
and Flair, grateful only to be free and unaware of
the rain that streamed over them both, buried her
face in his shirt and clung to him, feeling with relief
his arms around her, holding her safe. 'What on
earth did you run like that for?'

'I thought—you were so angry, I thought you—I
was scared,' she stammered. 'Oh, Luke——'

He stared down at her. Rain turned his hair a dull gold and flattened it against his head; drops quivered on his brows. Then, as if compelled by some outside power, he bent his head and laid his lips on hers. Flair felt a tingling in her stomach, a tingling that spread rapidly as fire through her body. Then she was responding to him, matching ardour with ardour. She slid her arms up round his neck, holding him close, straining her body against his. It doesn't matter what happens after this, her mind sang, it just doesn't matter. *This* is all that matters. And she didn't notice the rain that cascaded over them, so that they seemed to be standing beneath a tumbling waterfall; didn't notice that Luke's hand was wet as it slipped over her swelling breast. She only knew that whatever the conditions, wherever they might be, this was her place. And when her mind told her that it couldn't last, she pushed the thought away. If it didn't last, she would at least have had it. At that moment, that was all that mattered.

'Flair,' Luke muttered huskily at last, taking his lips from hers with reluctance. 'Flair, what are we doing to each other? Why do we keep fighting?'

'I—I don't understand,' she whispered, acutely conscious of the thumb that gently stroked her neck, sending shivers down her back.

'I'm not sure I understand myself.' He smiled crookedly. 'I've been fighting this ever since that day at the swimming-pool, Flair, didn't you realise that?' His fingers tightened a little, drawing her closer. 'Do you know what I mean?'

Wordlessly, Flair shook her head. The rain poured

over them, its pounding matched by the pounding of her blood.

'I swore I'd never say this to anyone,' Luke said quietly. 'When I saw you there, looking at me with those great green mermaid's eyes, and I knew what you were doing to me, I hated you for it, can you believe that? I didn't want it to happen—but I couldn't help myself. Whenever you came close——' he groaned and buried his face in her breasts, 'I wanted to drive you away. When I sent you back from the island, I spent the rest of that day cursing myself.'

That wasn't Roxanne's version, Flair thought. But the American girl had no place here and the thought faded as quickly as it had come. She looked up into Luke's eyes and her heart turned over at the expression in them.

'What—what is it you want to say?' she murmured, half aware of the answer, half afraid of it, yet knowing that the moment had come for absolute truth between the two of them.

Luke smiled at her, a smile that held a depth of tenderness that she had never dreamed of finding. His fingers traced the lines of her face and then his hand slipped round to the back of her head as if to hold her ready for his kiss. When he spoke, his voice was low.

'Flair, I love you. I can't go on like this, fighting you, driving you away. I want you with me, now and for always, by my side, sharing my life, my ambitions, my bed. Is that what you want too, Flair? Tell me it is, darling—tell me *now*!'

Flair stared at him, unable to take in what he

said. The surging of her blood blotted out all other sound, all other sensation. He *loved* her. He wanted to marry her. It couldn't be true. . . .

'Flair?' Luke said urgently, and she closed her eyes and nodded.

'I love you, Luke,' she whispered, and sighed with delight as his lips touched hers at last.

Luke's kiss, at first tender, became more demanding, and happiness flooded Flair's body as she eagerly moulded herself against him, moving herself against his hardness, arching her back so that her breasts thrust against the wall of his chest. It was as if she had forgotten how to breathe, had no need to, as if Luke's mouth breathed his own vitality into her, filling her with a sensuous desire so powerful it shocked her and left her gasping. As his lips left hers to travel fiercely over her face, nipping gently at her earlobes, burning their path down her neck to her breasts, she let her own hands move over him, unbuttoning his shirt so that she could feel the soft golden hairs, slide her arms right round him and pull him nearer still; and gasped as she discovered that at some point her own shirt had been unfastened, and skin met skin.

'Luke,' she whispered. 'Luke, I love you. . . .'

Slowly, still kissing her as if he couldn't stop, Luke drew away from her. He glanced down at their streaming bodies and smiled. 'We're soaked right through,' he muttered. 'Do you mind?'

Eyes dancing, Flair shook her head. 'I'll need to change, though—get out of these wet clothes. . . .'

'You know what you are?' he muttered, pulling her close again and fiddling with the waistband of her jeans. 'You're a she-devil. Did Lucifer have a wife, do you know?'

In unspoken agreement, they moved back towards the car, pausing to kiss at every other step, their arms closely entwined about each other's waists. Flair's heart hammered as they reached the wagon and Luke opened the door. It was the work of a moment, she knew, to release the back seat, making a wide, comfortable bed. She turned wide eyes on him, imagining the final climax of their love, here in the strange semi-darkness of the tree's hollow trunk with the sound of water foaming at its roots. Shivering with anticipation, she allowed him to slide her wet jeans down her legs; watched, trembling, as he stripped himself, then turned to her with darkened eyes and a grave face.

And then she realised that the rain had stopped, as abruptly as it began. The sunlight broke through and knifed through the shining trees, streaking the forest with shafts of dazzling gold and bringing colour even to the darkness of the hollow tree where they stood. And from somewhere along the track floated the sound of voices—laughing, chattering voices. A sound that grew louder and closer every moment.

Luke swore and grabbed at their cases, pulling out dry clothes and handing them to Flair so that she could hastily drag them on. As she did so, he scrambled quickly into a pair of shorts and a loose shirt, then slid into the driving seat and held Flair's door open for her.

'Tourists,' he said in tones of deep disgust. 'Coming this way, too. They certainly know how to pick their moments!' He grinned ruefully at her. 'Still, I suppose we could have picked somewhere less public.'

Giving her a quick, hard kiss, he started the car. Within moments they were bumping back along the track, passing a group of middle-aged tourists on the way and slowing down to round their coach at the entrance to the narrow road. Then they were back on the tarmac and Flair, shaken and trembling, was beginning to wonder if it had really happened.

'Sorry about that, Flair,' Luke murmured then, resting his hand lightly on her thigh. 'Let's continue our—discussion—somewhere a little more private, shall we?'

CHAPTER SEVEN

THE rest of the morning passed in a haze of happiness. There didn't seem to be any need to discuss anything; not yet. It was enough just to be together in this new world, this world that had turned upside down and proved to be so much, much better and brighter than the old one. They drove quietly along the empty roads, surrounded by the beauty of the forests with their giant trees and swarming flowers, and talked, letting each other see into their hearts and minds. Flair told Luke about her parents, how they had never been really happy together, though they had never quarrelled much, and how when Jeff had had the opportunity to come to Australia to do the work he loved Susan had decided to stay behind.

'She'd just got the chance of this headship, you see,' Flair explained, 'and it was just what she'd always dreamed of. I think she was relieved that she didn't have to worry about Dad. It seemed the right thing for both of them.'

'And was it for you?' Luke asked. 'Seeing your family split up like that—having to say goodbye to your father and share your mother with two or three hundred other girls?'

Flair shrugged. 'I did miss Dad a lot. But I was happy enough, I suppose. I didn't have much time to think about it. They keep you on the move at boarding schools, you know!'

Luke was silent for a while, then he said quietly: 'But from what you've said, I get the impression your mother was more headmistress than mum. Or am I wrong?'

'No, you're not,' Flair answered, surprised at his perception. 'She was—especially during term, there couldn't be any favouritism. And during the holidays I suppose she found it hard to switch off. But she was always like that really. Much more the career woman than mother or wife.'

'And her daughter?' Luke asked softly. 'How do you feel, Flair, about being a wife and mother? Or does your career mean more to you, too?'

Flair thought for a moment. Then she said: 'No. Not any more. There was a time when I thought it did—when I thought my career was more important than marriage could ever be. But that was before I met you.' She let her hand rest on his knee, feeling the hard muscles of his thigh. 'I had to fight too, Luke. I didn't *want* to give up all the ideas I'd had for so long. But now——'

'Now?' he murmured, dropping his hand on to hers and moving his fingers slowly, sensuously, so that tiny thrills ran like electric shocks up her arm and into her body.

'Now I just want to be with you,' she said softly. 'For the rest of my life.'

Luke talked then, telling her about his own background, and as he talked Flair began to understand his apparently hard attitude to women. No wonder, she thought as she listened, that he'd seen women as toys, to be played with and used but not to be treated seriously; not to be allowed into his heart. Her only wonder was that Luke, too, had turned his ideas upside down and allowed himself to love her.

'Mum left when I was three,' he said, keeping his eyes on the road that ran so straight ahead of them. 'I suppose there'd been problems—but I never knew, I was too young. I don't even remember her properly—just one or two vague pictures. All I do know is that it ruined Dad. I don't think he was ever the same again. He never stopped loving her, you see. He lost heart for everything else—the business, me, living itself. He did his best, I can't say he didn't—but I always knew he was eating his heart out for something, or someone, else. He died when I was sixteen, and it might sound crazy to say it was of a broken heart, but I believe it was. He just hung on to make sure I was old enough to fend for myself, you see, then he went.'

'Oh, Luke,' Flair said sympathetically, 'that's terrible! And you never heard any more from your mother?'

'Not a word. She just didn't want to know, I guess. Found someone else—may have a dozen other kids by now. Frankly, I don't care.'

They sat in silence for a while after that. Flair was thinking deeply about what Luke had told her. It obviously hadn't been easy for him to tell her that story. She guessed it was something he rarely talked about and probably wouldn't mention again. But she didn't believe him when he said he didn't care about his mother. He cared a lot—and he was still hurt. That was what had embittered him, what had turned him against women. That was why he hadn't wanted to love her.

But things would be different now, she promised silently. From now on, she would teach him that women *could* be relied on, trusted, loved. From now on the bitterness would be assuaged from his soul.

They didn't have time to stop much for sightseeing that day—Luke was anxious to get back to Perth by nightfall. He paused merely long enough to show Flair the Natural Bridge, a series of huge slabs of rock that formed a bridge over the roaring waves of a rocky cove, and the Gap nearby—a deep cleft in sheer cliffs, down which Flair was fascinated and horrified to see two climbers hanging like flies above the surging foam. Then they sped on to Albany, where Flair caught only glimpses of the brig *Amity*, the replica of the ship that had brought the first European settlers to Western Australia, and the Dog Rock, like a huge labrador sitting by the road in the middle of the town. It didn't take long for Luke to see what he wanted of the motel site and to complete his business with the local men who were to be working on it; and then, after a quick lunch, they were on their way back to Perth, going this time through the Stirling ranges.

'You don't mind us rushing back, do you, Flair?' Luke asked as they passed through the tumble of mountain scenery that was so different from the long straight roads and forests of the Leeuwin Way. 'We'll come again and we'll take it easier next time. Only now that we've settled ourselves, there are quite a few things I want to get straightened out back in Perth. I want us to be married as soon as possible, my darling—but there are some loose ends want tying up first.'

Flair smiled back at him, loving the strong, clean lines of his profile. Of course she didn't mind—she didn't mind anything, provided it meant that she and Luke could be together. Though she did wish that he'd stop, just for a few minutes, and kiss her again. . . . She felt weak as the memory of his kisses invaded her mind. She let her hand rest on his thigh and he turned and smiled at her. But he didn't suggest stopping.

It was late evening when they arrived back in Perth. Jeff was out again, to Flair's disappointment—she had looked forward to telling him their news, knowing how it would please him. She turned to Luke, expecting him to suggest a meal either here or at the hotel. But instead he took her in his arms and said gently: 'I think we'd better call it a day now, Flair, don't you? You must be exhausted after that long drive—and I do need to catch up on some work before I go to bed. A quick supper and then bed is what I suggest for you!'

'Can't you stay and have something with me?' she murmured, nuzzling her face into his neck, and felt his throat vibrate as he laughed softly.

'I could, but if I did I don't think I'd ever leave! Look, we'll have all the time in the world soon, I promise you. I'll see you in the morning—as early as you like to make it.' He kissed her and Flair felt her bones melt. She clung to him, responding with all the ardour that was in her, all the ardour she had been afraid to unleash before. But after a few minutes, he held her away from him and said regretfully: 'I really must go, love. Don't make it too hard for me.'

Flair shook her head. 'I'll see you in the morning, then.'

'At the crack of dawn,' Luke promised with a wicked grin, and he was gone.

But although Flair did as she'd been told, made herself an omelette and went to bed to dream of Luke so vividly that she woke convinced he was there with her, she did not see him in the morning. And by the time they did meet, everything had changed.

There was a small box waiting on Flair's desk when she arrived at the hotel next morning. She eyed it with excitement and some doubt. It looked like a ring-box—but why was it waiting on her desk? And where was Luke?

'Mr Seager's had to go over to the island suddenly,' Janet told her when she enquired. 'He had a message very early from the men who're starting work there today. Some snag—but he didn't seem too worried. Said he'd be back later this afternoon with any luck.'

'I see.' Flair wandered back into her own office and looked at the box again. Presumably Luke had intended to give it to her this morning, and having been called away had left it for her to find. She wasn't sure she liked getting engaged this way and wondered why he couldn't have left it until he got back. But maybe he thought it would make up for her own disappointment; maybe he wanted to find her wearing it when he did come back.

She opened the box and looked at the ring inside. Her lips parted and a tiny sigh of pure delight escaped them.

A large, egg-shaped opal glowed up at her, its colours streaked with blue and red. She took it out and slipped it on her finger. It fitted exactly, and she turned it about, gazing in wonder at the depth of its colouring, the mystery of its patterns. Someone had dug this out of the raw earth, and somewhere Luke had found it and thought it right for her. And so it was—exactly right. But where and when had he bought it? When had he decided that he wanted to marry her?

A sound startled her and she looked up sharply to see Roxanne in the doorway, watching her. Hastily she slipped the box into the drawer of her desk, but she knew that Roxanne had seen and the other girl's face sharpened with an avid curiosity. She took a step forward and Flair said quickly: 'Hello, Roxanne. Did you want something?'

'Nothing that you can help me with, honey,' the American girl drawled. 'I was hoping to see Luke.'

'I'm afraid he's not here,' Flair said calmly. 'He's gone over to Blue Island.'

'Away *again?*' Roxanne pouted. She was looking exceptionally beautiful this morning in a low-cut scarlet sundress, Flair thought, able to feel magnanimous towards the other girl now. 'That man's always dashing off somewhere.'

'It's his job,' Flair said smoothly. 'I expect your father's just the same.'

'Oh, Pop——' Roxanne shrugged. 'He just lives for work. But Luke's different, isn't he? *He* knows how to enjoy himself as well. Or maybe you wouldn't know much about that, Miss Pattison—being just his assistant.'

Flair said nothing and began to sort the post, hoping that Roxanne would go. Then she became aware of the brunette's scrutiny and glanced up to see Roxanne's sultry eyes fixed on her hands—on the opal ring she was wearing on her engagement finger.

'Say, that's really something.' Roxanne bent closer to look. 'A real opal, huh? You got yourself engaged, Miss Pattison?' The curiosity was naked in her eyes as they flicked up over Flair's burning face.

Well, everyone would know sooner or later. It was just that she would have preferred Roxanne *not* to be the first to hear their news. With a tiny sigh, Flair said simply: 'Yes, I am, as a matter of fact.'

'You *are*?' Roxanne's voice sounded almost genuinely pleased, though it was mainly, Flair supposed, because she herself no longer seemed to present a threat to the American girl's plans. 'And who's the lucky man? Anyone I know?' Clearly, she didn't expect it to be—she wouldn't 'know' anyone of what she might think of as Flair's circle.

Flair hesitated. For some reason which she couldn't analyse, she didn't want to tell Roxanne that she was engaged to Luke. She felt almost superstitious about it as if it might bring bad luck. But there was nothing else for it and, reluctantly, she admitted the truth.

Roxanne stared at her. Her mouth opened a little, her face turned pale. For a moment she seemed bereft of speech. Then an ugly expression crept into her eyes and they narrowed almost to slits. Flair saw her whole body tense as the dull, angry colour flooded back into her face.

'*Luke?*' Roxanne said at last, and her voice was rasping and harsh. 'You're engaged to *Luke?*'

'Yes, that's right.' Flair wished the girl would go away. It was unpleasant to stand here and watch her rage; almost frightening. She had never seen anyone look quite like that before.

Roxanne gave a short, unpleasant laugh. 'You must be mad! Or course you're not engaged to Luke. Why, he's as good as engaged to *me.*'

'I'm sorry, Roxanne,' Flair said patiently, 'but he's not. He asked me to marry him yesterday.'

'Yesterday? Then there must be some reason for it.' The tall, voluptuous body swayed angrily up and down the room, the red material of her dress swirling like a flame about her. 'He didn't mean it, you may be sure of that. Luke means to marry *me*—and I sure mean to marry *him.*' She reached the window and swung round. 'Why, he wouldn't risk everything just now—he thinks too much of his business for that. Isn't it what he puts first, always? Isn't it what he's worked for all these years? You don't think he's going to start courting a little nobody like you at *this* stage, do you? It could ruin everything—and Luke's not going to see that happen. No, there's some other reason for it—and I bet I know just what it is, too.'

'Roxanne, please—there's no mistake, no *reason*—Luke and I are in love and we're going to be married——'

'*In love?*' The American's eyes widened and she laughed. 'Luke Seager in love? Why, he doesn't know the meaning of the word! Oh, *sex*, yes, he knows all about *that*—he's taken some trouble to learn, and anyway he's the kinda man who doesn't need much teaching. But *love*—that doesn't come into his calculations.'

'It does now,' said Flair, trying not to let the American girl's scorn shake her own conviction that Luke loved her.

'Well, it's a new line, but I guess he thought it was the only one to take.' Roxanne looked her up and down. 'The simple little English rose—yeah, it figures. But it'll never happen—and if you want to save yourself from a whole lot of misery, you'll take that from me now and get out while you can.'

Flair stared at her, her heart suddenly beating fast.

'I don't know what you're talking about,' she said. 'Luke——'

'*Luke!*' Roxanne repeated scathingly. 'You've really got your rose-tinted glasses on, haven't you? Luke's going to marry *me*, get that? And I'll tell you why. He's going to marry me because that's the only way Pop's going to agree to this merger going through. Oh yeah, they both want it—but Pop can manage without and if I don't get Luke, it's no go. Pop's always given me anything I want, you see. And I want Luke, I don't mind telling you that.'

'But yesterday——' Flair began, and Roxanne interrupted her.

'Yesterday nothing. I told you, there's got to be some reason. He's not committed to you, is he? No one else knows this tremendous news?'

'No, I——'

'And if I'm guessing right you'd only just found that ring when I walked in, hadn't you? Luke never put it on your finger himself.'

Flair stared down at the opal, glowing on her finger. *Had* it been meant for an engagement ring? If Luke had been here, would he have slipped it on to just that finger? Or ... she grew cold ... had it been intended as a—a consolation present? Compensation for something he'd never intended, for a moment's madness.

Committed—Flair felt totally committed to Luke. But did he to her? They hadn't made love yet, not fully. Indeed, for the last part of the journey Luke had seemed almost to avoid any opportunity to do so. He hadn't taken the chance to stop in the Sterling ranges; he hadn't even come through the door of her father's house last night. Her eyes suddenly misted with tears, she looked up at Roxanne.

'I don't believe you,' she said, struggling to convince herself. 'You're just jealous—you're just trying to hurt me.'

Roxanne shrugged her lovely shoulders. 'Okay, honey,' she said indifferently. 'If that's the way you want it—but you'll find out. Just ask your father, that's all. Ask him why his contract with Seager Hotels has been cancelled——'

'*Cancelled?*'

'Ask him why all his work for the Blue Island project is being reviewed and finished off by *our* architect—Ryan's. Ask him why he's not being kept on for the Albany motel or any of Luke's other places that are being improved and enlarged, let alone anything new. Ask him why, if it's not because Luke's going into the merger in a big way and he's agreed to employ Pop's designers.' She stopped and her narrowed eyes took in Flair's white face and huge, shocked eyes. '*That's* why Luke Seager's asked you to marry him,' she said cruelly. 'He doesn't want Jeff Pattison suing him for a broken contract. And he knows you're the apple of your daddy's eye—just like I am mine. As long as you and Luke are engaged, Jeff won't lift a finger—but as soon as that merger's signed and settled, believe you me, honey, your engagement's going to be *off*—and it'll be little Roxanne who's wearing a long white dress and walking up the aisle of St George's Cathedral.'

She paused once more and looked for a long moment at the opal ring on Flair's finger.

'Maybe he'll let you keep it for a souvenir,' she murmured silkily. She gave Flair one last glance from eyes that smouldered with a mixture of scorn, pity and complete certainty. Then, with a movement that reminded Flair of a great cat after a kill, she turned and walked coolly from the room, closing the door behind her.

Flair stood where she was, unable to move. Her heart was beating so hard she felt that it was coming right into her throat. Her body felt cold, in spite of the warmth of the day. She shuddered and moved to pick up her jacket, but her limbs moved stiffly, as if she had suddenly grown old.

The opal ring still glowed, the deep red of its centre looking like a heart of fire. She stared at it. It had been there such a short time—less than half an hour, her watch told her, though it seemed much, much longer.

Slowly, she drew it from her finger, opened the drawer and put it back into its little box. Whether Roxanne's accusations had been true or not, she

could not wear it again until she had seen Luke.
Until he himself had slipped it on to her finger.

Trying to keep her misery at bay, Flair worked
steadily through the rest of the morning. She refused lunch, asking Janet only for coffee when the
secretary came in to say that she was going in a
few minutes, and as she drank it she thought over
Roxanne's words and admitted to herself that they
could well be true. She had been surprised, taken
aback, by Luke's declaration of love—up to then she
had thought him alternately indifferent to and
attracted by her. But his attraction had only been
physical, a kind of lust; she had sensed that from the
beginning, even when she had acknowledged her
own love. And now it seemed to be confirmed.

She bent her head and rested it on her hand,
allowing the full weight of her unhappiness to sweep
over her. If only she could *hate* him! But underneath
all the doubts, all the bitterness that she could have
been so taken in, she knew that her own love was as
strong and true as ever. And that made the pain so
much harder to bear.

Was it all true? Was Luke just stringing her along
to prevent Jeff from suing him? There was only one
way to find out. With a quick glance at her watch,
Flair saw that her father should be leaving his own
office now for lunch. If she hurried, she might still
just catch him. . . .

Jeff's office was near the shopping malls, a little
farther down St George's Terrace from the Seager
Hotel. He was just coming out when Flair hurried
up to the door, and his face broke into a smile

at the sight of her.

'Flair! What a nice surprise. It seems a long time since we met—we've been like Box and Cox at home lately, haven't we?'

'I thought we might have a quick lunch together,' said Flair, and he nodded.

'A nice idea—it'll have to be quick, though, I've a client coming at two and he's *always* punctual. Look, there's a small restaurant in London Court I go to when I'm in a hurry.'

He led her into the narrow arcade built like an old-fashioned London street. Tiny shops selling gifts, souvenirs, books and clothes, lined the sides. Jeff turned aside into a small restaurant, cooled with air-conditioning, and found a quiet table.

'I recommend the lasagne,' he said, handing Flair a menu. 'And they do some especially luscious tortes here, too. . . .'

'That will be fine.' Flair handed the menu back. 'Dad, I want to talk to you. There's something I've got to know—something I heard this morning.'

Jeff glanced at her, then turned to give his order to the waitress. It wasn't a licensed restaurant, so they had fresh orange juice, which came in large tumblers and tasted delicious. Once they were settled, Flair tried again.

'Dad, is it true——'

'Ssh,' he interrupted, 'here's our lasagne. You see why I come here when I'm in a hurry? It's so quick—and good, too. Not to mention cheap,' he added with a smile, and Flair looked at him in consternation.

'Dad, you're not hard up?'

'No, of course not—it was just a joke.' But she

wasn't convinced. How much would it mean to her father if he lost the Seager contract? Quite a lot, it must do. Seager's must be the biggest contract he had—it took up nearly all his time. Lose that, and what would be left? Very little.

'You aren't eating,' he reminded her gently. 'Flair, you're looking like a terrified rabbit. Whatever it is, it can't be that bad. What's happened?'

Flair took a deep breath. The lasagne cooled on her plate, but she ignored it. She said in a low voice:

'Dad, I've got to know. Is it true that your contract with Luke has been cancelled?'

Jeff lowered his fork and looked at her. His face was grey, even his eyes seemed to have lost some of their colour, she noticed, but she wasn't sure if it had been like that before or not. She'd been too absorbed to look at him properly.

'*Has* it?' she repeated urgently.

'Who told you that?'

'Roxanne did. It doesn't matter. Dad——'

'*Roxanne* did?' His eyebrows raised. 'Oh well, I suppose there's not much that young woman can't worm out of her besotted father. And I'm not really one to talk about being besotted, anyway. But I did ask that it be kept quiet.'

'*You* did? But why—oh, I suppose you thought it would spoil things for me. Well, you needn't have worried about that. I can get another job any day, I——'

'It wasn't just your job,' Jeff interrupted, and Flair stared at him.

'You mean you thought—you thought Luke and

I——' The idea seemed almost incredible now. She pushed away the thought of the opal ring, of Luke's proposal in the streaming rain under the tingle tree. 'Dad, he's the most arrogant, hateful, woman-hating man I've ever had the misfortune to meet! Oh, I can see he'd attract *some* women—but not me! You can rest assured about *that*. I hope that if and when I ever do marry—and I'm not at all sure I'll ever want to—I'll be lucky enough to find a man who's a lot more sensitive and caring than Luke Seager. Otherwise I'll be happy to stay a spinster.'

'Oh, Flair,' her father said, smiling, 'you sound so much like your mother—and you don't know what you're talking about. Because you're *not* like her. You're not cold and self-sufficient. You're not the career girl you think you are. You're the sort of person who needs someone to share life with—a partner, to love and be loved by. Someone to laugh with, someone to cry with. You've got a warm, loving nature, Flair, and it would be a crime to let it go to waste.' He paused and finished his lasagne. 'And you're wrong about Luke, too. He's a fine man. There's a lot you don't understand, Flair.'

'I wouldn't be too sure of that, Dad,' said Flair, her voice shaky. 'I've learned a lot in these past few days. . . . I'm sorry, I'm not really hungry. Do you mind if I don't finish this? And I ought to be getting back now, anyway—there's any amount of work to do at the hotel.'

Her throat choked with tears, she pushed her plate away and almost ran from the restaurant, while Jeff looked after her with a worried frown creasing his tired brow.

CHAPTER EIGHT

LUKE returned late that afternoon. He was sunburnt from his sea trip and day on the island. He came into the office like a breath of fresh sea breeze and grasped Flair round the waist as she stood at a filing cabinet, sweeping her off her feet before she could speak.

'Flair! Sorry I had to dash off like that this morning—goodness, I've missed you! Just didn't seem right without that little elfin face of yours and that gorgeous smile. Come on, give me a kiss and tell me how you liked the ring I left for you. Does it fit? We can soon have it altered if not.'

Flair looked up and met his eyes. For a moment her heart twisted and she wanted to forget all her pain and doubt, to fling herself into his arms and let the world go by. But she couldn't do that, she reminded herself. If Roxanne were right, it was all a farce—all a huge lie, an act. Luke didn't really love her—didn't love anybody—but he was going to marry Roxanne anyway. The ring meant nothing; his words yesterday meant nothing.

Luke's brows gathered in a puzzled frown. 'Flair?' he said questioningly. 'Flair, what is it? You look worried.'

'Worried?' she repeated. 'Worried? Now why should I look worried? The world's my oyster, isn't it? I've got you, so I've got everything. Nothing else matters, does it.'

'You don't sound as if you mean that,' he said. 'Flair, what is it? What's happened?'

'That's what I'd like to know,' she retorted. 'You tell me! Just what *has* happened, Luke—have we got engaged or have I been taken for one long ride? I'd like to know—not that it's really important, you understand, but a girl does like to have some idea of where she stands.'

Luke's hands fell away from her and he took a step back. His face was genuinely puzzled—or was it just another stage in his act? she wondered bitterly. He certainly knew how to put it on.

'Look, I don't know what idea you've got into your head,' he began, 'but I wish you'd give me some clue. Or am I supposed to guess? Because I'm not really in the mood for games, Flair, I warn you.'

'And I am, of course!' she blazed. 'I just love spending the whole day wondering just what you're up to—getting a hint here, a clue there—piecing it all together for myself. Well, all right, Luke, just so *you* don't have to suffer the same way, here it is! You don't love me at all—you don't love anyone but Luke Seager—and you don't mean to marry me either. It's Roxanne, isn't it—*she's* the lucky girl who's going to be Mrs Luke Seager. Well, she'll need her luck, that's all I can say. She's welcome to you!'

Luke's face hardened and she felt a tremor of fear as she caught his glance like a blast of icy wind. Almost automatically she put up a hand to ward him off as he moved nearer; but he merely gripped both her wrists in iron fingers and rasped at her:

'And just where did you get all these cock-eyed ideas, Flair? You'd better tell me.' His fingers tightened so that she gasped with pain, but his eyes were cruel and she knew she could expect no mercy.

'She told me! Roxanne told me herself—she said the merger wouldn't go through unless you married her, it's all virtually settled——'

'I see.' His face was grim, his eyes like chips of stone. 'Very interesting. And just why am I getting myself engaged to you, then? It seems a little tactless, to say the least.'

'Because of Dad,' Flair gasped, tears brimming from her eyes. 'Because you've cancelled his contract and you don't want him to sue you. Because you're going to use Ryan's architects. You—you've gone back on your word, you've wrecked his livelihood, and you've made sure it won't affect you in the slightest by pretending you love me. You know he wouldn't do anything to hurt me, and you're taking advantage of it.'

'And you really think that?' Luke asked, his tones silky and dangerous.

'How can I believe otherwise?' she flung at him. 'It all fits in, doesn't it—your behaviour, the way you wouldn't stop and make love to me yesterday once you were sure of me, the way you just left that ring here for me to find. And I know it's true, anyway—about Dad. I've seen him—I asked him.'

Luke dragged her against him. She struggled, but it was useless. His breath was warm on her face as he spoke again, and his voice was hard and grating.

'You've *seen* him? What did he say?'

'That—that it was true. Luke, you're hurting me——'

'I'll hurt you a damn sight more before this is

finished,' he gritted. 'Go on. What did he say? What did he tell you?'

'Just that it was true.' Now that she came to think of it, she hadn't given him much chance to say anything else, and he'd rather successfully changed the subject, but she wasn't telling Luke that. 'He told me the truth, what else is there?'

Luke grunted, but his grip on her didn't relax. 'And you believe this too? That I've broken your father's contracts, that I'm going to marry Roxanne all to be sure of the merger? That's the way you see it, is it?'

'Yes—*yes!*' Flair gazed up at him through a haze of tears. 'What else *can* I believe?'

'I don't know,' said Luke, staring down at her. 'I really don't know. Obviously, you won't believe anything *I* tell you, anyway. Well, I guess our engagement's off, then.' He let her go suddenly and shrugged while Flair staggered and put her hand to her head. 'That didn't last long, did it? Can't say I'm not sorry, even though I am such a bastard. I reckon I'd have enjoyed making love to you.' He turned suddenly and came nearer with a swift movement, a wicked gleam in his eye. 'In fact, that was one of the things you complained about, wasn't it? The fact that I *didn't* make love to you. Well, that's one thing I *can* put right!'

Flair caught her breath. He couldn't mean it—he couldn't be intending to—but already his arms were around her, hard and strong. He lifted her easily, carrying her like a baby, and she felt him swing her across the office to the door that led to his own private quarters. She kicked and cried out as he strode across the lounge and flung open the farthest door; a door she'd never been through; the door that led to his bedroom. . . .

'*Luke!*' she panted, struggling and clawing at his back—the only part she could reach, since his arms were pinning hers close against his sides. 'Luke, no—*please!* Just let me go—let me leave now—Luke——'

'Let you leave?' he snarled, throwing her down on the wide bed and standing over her as she lay sprawled on the soft duvet. 'Let you walk out of here after the things you've said—oh no, Flair, you don't get away with it that easily. You said you wanted me to make love to you, remember? You were disappointed that I didn't yesterday—oh yes, I know, but for some strange reason I thought you wanted to be respected, if you like that quaint old-fashioned phrase—I thought you'd rather wait. And I knew that if I did stop, if I just got you into my arms where no one else could see, there'd be no holding back. I've wanted you long and badly enough, Flair Pattison. What you've been doing to me ought to go down in the books as refined torture. And you're not getting away with it—whatever else happens or doesn't happen between you and me, I'm going to make damned sure of that!'

Flair lay paralysed, her eyes wide and green, watching in terror as he locked the door. The room was large and dominantly masculine, decorated in shades of brown, black and gold. It seemed to fit Luke like his immaculate suits, like the well-cut jeans and silk shirt he wore now. Her body quivered as she watched him approach the bed again. She wanted desperately to get up and run, useless though it might be; but a strange, heavy languor swept over her, keeping her on the bed, dulling her mind. The only thing in sharp focus was Luke, and she was beginning to realise that she was powerless to resist.

He was beside her now, leaning over her, his arms on each side of her so that she was pinned where she lay. His blue eyes glittered with the brilliance and hardness of sapphires. She smelt the fresh tang of his body and closed her eyes, turning her head to one side. Strong fingers turned it back, and held it there while his lips came down on hers.

Flair's senses swam. She tried to resist, to close her mouth against him, but his lips parted hers firmly, inexorably. She lay stiff, trying to ignore the effect produced by his searching mouth, trying to pretend that the hands that moved with practised ease over her body meant nothing, that their touch was alien to her. She tried, desperately, to think of something else.

Luke moved so that he was lying beside her, half over her, his body warm on hers. His mouth left hers and moved slowly, sensuously across her face, closing her eyelids, nipping at her ears. He bent his head and blazed a trail down the slim column of her throat, coming to rest on the hollow where the pulse beat fast and jumpily.

Almost against her will, Flair's arms crept up around his neck, drawing him closer. She had very nearly stopped thinking. Once again, she and Luke were in a world of their own, a world of languorous movement and touch and sensuality. She rubbed her face against his hair and sighed in the fragrance of it, that essentially masculine scent that seemed to belong exclusively to him. She moved her body against his, feeling her breasts swell and harden at the contact. Her thighs pressed against his; she felt the hardness of his contours against her own softness.

Luke muttered something in a thick, husky voice. He unbuttoned her blouse and pulled it apart, burying his face in her breasts. Somehow, her bra was undone too, and he tugged it away and stayed for a moment looking down at her.

'My God,' he muttered, 'you're lovely, Flair.' He lowered his face again, biting gently at her nipples, covering her breasts with tiny kisses, moulding them in his hands. Flair twisted closer to him, arching her back in invitation. She pulled at his own shirt, spreading her fingers over the golden hairs of his chest, then pulled him down again so that their skins met.

'Luke,' she whispered, heedless of all her former determination, aware only of her desperate need for him, a primitive urge that had nothing to do with reason. 'Luke—love me—Luke—Luke—Luke. . . .'

'Love you?' he muttered, undoing the waistband of her skirt with rapid fingers and pulling it away. 'Is it what you really want, Flair? We've been this far before, you know—don't turn back again now unless you really mean it.'

'Love me!' she begged. His hands were running up and down her body, from neck to knee and she shuddered with longing. He lifted himself from her and twisted round, bending to nuzzle her feet, kissing each toe in turn, running his lips up her instep. Flair moved her other foot against his face, delighting in the feel of it, and felt his lips on the sole. Then, one arm outspread so that his hand could cover her breast, he let his mouth explore the length of her leg, tauntingly, provocatively from toe to thigh. Flair felt her entire body tingle. She clutched at his hand and arm with both hands; then let her arms slide round him as he came back to claim her mouth once more.

They lay entwined, rocking to and fro together, mouths joined in a kiss that was deeper than any yet. Flair felt contentment flow through her, warm and comforting. Surely it had all been a terrible mistake. Luke did love her. He must do. Just as she loved him. Everything would be—it *must* be—all right.

'Luke,' she whispered against his lips, 'I'm sorry about—about all that, I should have known better than to believe Roxanne. But you *will* put things right with Dad, won't you?'

He stiffened at once and Flair realised with a sinking heart that she had spoken too soon. She felt him draw away from her, and when he spoke his voice was cool.

'No, Flair, I'm sorry—I can't do that.'

'But why not?' Her eyes looked into his, green clashing with blue. 'What's he done, Luke? Isn't his work good enough?'

'His work's fine, Flair, you know that. But I can't do anything about those contracts. I've told you.'

'But why *not*?'

'I can't. It's not just up to me, it's——'

'Not up to you? Then who *is* it up to?' He didn't answer and she cried: 'It's Ryan, isn't it? It's all to do with that merger, just as Roxanne said! Oh, Luke, why won't you see sense? Why can't you be satisfied? What does it *matter* about the merger—don't you have enough money? Is it just plain greed?'

Luke said nothing. His eyes narrowed and Flair flinched away, suddenly afraid that he was going to hit her. Her previous fears—fears she had only in the last day laughed at and thought foolish—came flooding back and she was aware of his strength and power.

Luke spoke at last, his voice flat.

'All right, Flair, get up. Get dressed, and then get out.'

'Get—*out?*' Her eyes were huge green pools in her white face. 'But——'

'Okay,' he said, 'you win. You never did want me to make love to you, did you, not really? Oh, your body wants it—you can't fool me about that. But you yourself—you're just stringing me along again, same as you always did. Up to the door, then slam it in my face. So that's it. I won't be taken in again.'

'Luke, I didn't——'

'It's this big innocent act that always gets me!' he exploded. 'The big wide eyes, the pained voice. "Oh, Luke, I never meant it like that," ' he minced. 'Like hell you didn't! It's the same old story, isn't it? I was right at the start—you're just a tease. And did I fall for it! I must want my head read.' He turned and paced over to the window. 'You don't really care about your father at all. It's just a blind, just something to use to break things up. Well, you've done it. And it's for the last time, you'd better believe *that*. From now on, Luke Seager steers very, very clear of little Flair Pattison.'

Flair wrapped herself in the duvet and ran across the room towards him. She didn't know now what she believed—she only knew that somehow this misunderstanding *must* be cleared up. But as she reached him, Luke whipped round and said savagely:

'I warn you, Flair, if I touch you now I won't answer for the consequences. Do you want to drive me mad?' He looked her up and down. 'Just what did they teach you at that posh English boarding school anyway?' he sneered. 'How to destroy your man in three easy lessons? You've really got it coming to you, you know that?' His eyes burned into her while she stood there, clutching the duvet around her. Then, with a stifled groan, he dragged her towards him, swinging her off her feet to hold her against him. His teeth ground against her mouth as he swung her back to the bed and flung her down again, wrenching the duvet away from her near-naked body. She felt the full, hard weight of his body as he bore down upon her, and the cruel strength of his hands as he held her to him. The pressure of his mouth was almost unbearable and as he finally released her mouth she drew a sharp inward breath and turned her head away, gasping and sobbing.

Luke jerked his body away and stood up. When she opened her eyes he was standing fully dressed at the side of the bed, looking down at her with contempt in his eyes.

'That's just a taste, Flair,' he grated. 'Try me one more time and you get the full measure, no holds barred—so be warned!'

Flair closed her eyes again, letting the tears trickle

out from under the lids. She heard Luke move away; heard the door open and close; and rolled over on to her side, crying now in real earnest.

She wasn't quite sure what she was weeping for. Whether because she loved Luke, or because she hated him. Because he had humiliated her, or because she still, in spite of everything, wanted him.

She only knew that his behaviour towards her father had made it impossible ever to feel either the contented companionship that she had experienced only a day or two earlier, or the soaring rapture that she had known when he kissed her under the tingle tree. Nor, she thought unhappily, was she ever likely to experience them with any other man.

Whether she liked it or not, Luke had set his brand on her, and she would never be able to be free of him.

Jeff, clad only in shorts and a loose shirt, was sitting in his favourite chair reading the *West Australian* when Flair came in later that evening. He glanced up with a smile, and his eyes sharpened.

'Flair? What is it—you look exhausted.' He looked closer. 'And you've been crying, surely. Flair, what's happened?'

She gave him a faint smile. It had taken her a long time, in Luke's luxurious bathroom, to remove the worst of the tear-stains, and then she'd walked for an hour or more beside the river, hoping that the fresh air would do the trick. But time was the only thing that would reduce the puffiness of her eyes, and she wasn't surprised that her father had noticed them.

'It's all right, Dad. Nothing much has happened. It's just that—well, Luke and I had a bit of a row and I've left the job, that's all.'

'You've left the job? Left Luke?' Jeff's voice was distressed, and he ran his fingers through his hair as he always did when agitated. 'My dear——'

'Please, Dad, I don't want to talk about it.' She sank into a chair and let her head flop back. 'I just want to go to bed and sleep and sleep, and forget it all. It hasn't been easy.'

'I never realised you were unhappy——'

'Well, I hoped it might settle down in time. But it didn't and there it is.' She looked up at him. 'Don't sympathise Dad, for heaven's sake, or I'll start crying again.'

He looked doubtful, but said no more. Flair closed her eyes again and heard him go out to the kitchen and make tea. In a few minutes he was back with a steaming cup, which she took gratefully.

'What are you going to do now?' he asked at last. 'Take a holiday, or look for another job? You don't have to, you know. I shan't in the least mind if you decide to have a break. After all, you wouldn't even have started work now if Luke hadn't wanted you sooner than we'd arranged.'

'No ... I don't know.' Flair stirred her tea thoughtfully. 'I don't really feel like a holiday, somehow. I think I need some occupation, if only for a few weeks.' A thought occurred to her and she paused. 'As a matter of fact, I think I do know what I'll do. ... Dad, have you ever met Dougie and Lance Carnagy? At Augusta? They run a small hotel there—rather a shabby little place, but comfy.'

'Dougie and Lance?' said Jeff. 'I should say I have! Did you stay there on the way down south, then? Wish I'd known—I could have sent them a message. Rude, of course!' He twinkled at her. 'They're a fine pair. But you're not thinking of going down there, are you, Flair?'

'I don't know,' she answered honestly. 'But I just might. They were saying they needed a hand with the books and correspondence—even offered me a job. I know it was a joke really, but at the same time . . . I think it could be what I need just now, Dad. Something completely different—quiet, undemanding, out of the rat-race. It would give me time. Time to collect myself, if you like.'

Jeff looked at her gravely. 'I won't ask any questions,' he said, 'but it seems to me that there's a lot more behind this than simply leaving a job you don't like, or even an employer you don't get on with. If there's anything I can do to help, Flair. . . .'

She finished her tea and smiled at him.

'Not really. There's nothing anyone can do. But thanks for offering, all the same.' She stood up and stretched. 'Do you know, I feel better already. I'm going to have a long, luxurious bath and put on something soft and long and not quite respectable enough to go out in. Then I think I'll ring Dougie and Lance. Just to see if they've any vacancies for the next week or two.'

CHAPTER NINE

THE sea at Canal Rocks was sparkling blue, topped with mounds of white foam that looked like puffs of whipped cream. Flair sat above the water with Lance, watching the boiling waves hurl themselves at the rocks to spray high in a burst of glittering droplets and stream down over the red rock formations to return to their own element. The long, rugged reef that ran parallel with the shore and gave the rocks their name was hidden every few moments in a surge of green and blue and white as yet another roller made landfall from the Indian Ocean, and she was aware of a power and energy greater than any humans had yet devised.

'Enjoying it?' Lance asked softly, and she smiled and nodded at him. Inside, she was wondering ruefully if it was true; but she could not have said so to Lance. And in a strange way, she was enjoying it. Even though the beauty itself twisted her heart with pain, even though the man at her side wasn't the man she longed to be with, she wouldn't have missed it. The pain was all she had of Luke, she thought sadly. Missing him was the only form her love could take. And if that were the case, then she must cherish her pain and her loneliness, for without them she had nothing at all.

Flair had been with Dougie and Lance for almost three weeks now. She recalled their surprise when

she had rung them to make sure they could give her
a room. They had expected Luke to be coming with
her too; when she'd said not, there had been an odd
little silence at the other end of the line, until Dougie
said with obvious tact: 'Well, of course we'll be glad
to see you, girl. You come on down and we'll have
our best room ready for you. And maybe a little
book-keeping, too, since you're offering!'

It had been just what Flair needed, their casual
acceptance of her. Neither of them had asked any
questions, and if she had occasionally caught
Dougie's bright eyes watching her with curiosity, or
Lance looking at her with rather more fondness than
she wanted to encourage, neither of them had ever
expressed their feelings. In their company, relaxed
and undemanding, she could at last unwind and
come to terms with her own emotions.

'It's been real beaut having you here, Flair,'
Lance said at last. 'You make all the difference to
the place. I was thinking, maybe we could smarten
things up a bit. Paint up the chalets, get some better
furniture—you'd know the kind of thing. Enlarge it
a bit, even. What do you think?'

'I don't know, Lance,' Flair said slowly. 'Don't
you think it would lose its atmosphere? Oh, I
know you need to redecorate, but do you really
want to alter things too much? People like it as it
is.'

'Yeah, but Luke says you shouldn't stand still.
Progress, he says, that's what gets you on in the
world. And look at him! *He* wouldn't have let our
motel stay the way it is, not for a day. He'd have
had the place ripped out and started over fresh,

and it'd have been a real bonza place with all the rich folk coming to stay——'

'But is that what you *want?*' Flair interrupted. 'Yes, Luke probably *would* have done that, because that's the kind of place he runs. It's the thing he's good at.' The thing we're both good at, the thing we could have done together, she thought miserably. 'But you and Dougie—you wouldn't be happy doing that. Your motel is exactly right for you and for the people who come to stay here.'

'And you?' asked Lance, so quietly that she didn't hear him and he had to repeat it. 'Is it right for you, Flair?'

Flair realised what he was leading up to and her heart sank. She had thought that her lack of encouragement, her determination to keep things on a merely friendly footing, had got through to the tall, shy Australian at her side. Whatever Luke had thought of her, she knew she had never intended to hurt Lance.

'For me?' she said. 'I don't see how I come into it. I'm just staying for a while, helping you out and having a nice lazy time. Yes, just at the moment the motel is exactly right for me.'

'That's not what I meant.' Lance turned to her, his eyes dark and urgent and she knew that she must take him seriously. 'I mean for good. For life. Is it the kind of place you want to run? Or is that Luke's sort of place? Because——' he stopped and swallowed, and Flair felt deeply sorry for him '——because whatever it is *you* want, then that's what *I* want. And Dad'll go along with it.' He reached out and held her gently by the shoulders. 'Take time to think about it if you like, Flair, I'm not asking you to decide right now. Just remember—things'll be the way *you* want them. So say whatever you like.'

'Lance,' Flair said gently, 'just what is it you're saying? Are you offering me a job—asking me to stay on and help manage the motel if you expand it? Is that it?'

He frowned and shook his head. 'Of course not! Flair, you *must* know how I feel about you. I want you to marry me—I'm asking you to be my *wife*. Yeah, I'd like us to stay on at the motel and make a good thing of it—but if you want something different, okay, we'll think about that. You just have to say, Flair.'

Flair sighed. When Lance had asked her if she would like this trip up to Canal Rocks, she had thought it was to be nothing more than a day out. It hadn't occurred to her that he might be intending it as a romantic situation for a proposal. Wrapped up in her own unhappiness over Luke, she hadn't seen that Lance's admiration and fondness for her had deepened into something more.

She knew that she couldn't let it go any further. There was nothing for her with Lance, nothing for him with her, whatever he might think now. Easygoing as he was, good companions as they were, marriage could be nothing but disaster for them both. Love on one side just wasn't enough.

'Lance,' she said softly, 'I can't marry you. I'm sorry—but it wouldn't work.' She sighed. 'I wish I thought it could. You'd make such a good husband—kind, considerate, easygoing. Nice to be with. But——'

'But that isn't enough,' said Lance as she hesitated. 'Is that it?'

'Yes. Yes, that's it. I'm sorry, Lance.'

There was a long silence. They both stared at the swirling, eddying water. The boom of the waves on distant rocks filled their ears. The sea gushed between the rocks and surged almost to their feet.

'It's Luke, isn't it?' said Lance at last.

The name went through Flair like a spear and she couldn't repress an involuntary shiver. Was she never going to be free? she asked herself in anguish. Was his name always to have this effect on her?

'Yes,' she said, knowing that nothing less than the truth would do. 'Yes, it's Luke.'

'You're in love with him?' She nodded, and he asked: 'And what about him?'

Flair shrugged helplessly. 'I don't know. I don't know if he's even capable of love. I thought he was—but then I found out something else. Things I can't talk about, Lance.' She turned her face away, feeling a stab of jealousy at the involuntary vision of Roxanne standing with Luke at the altar of St George's Cathedral, and a shaft of anger at the recollection of what he had done to her father.

'Well, I guess that's it, then,' said Lance after a long moment. 'But—Flair——' His hand touched her gently on the arm—'I don't think I'm going to change either. And if you ever feel you need me—any way at all—you come right here and tell me so. You will, won't you?'

'Oh, Lance,' Flair sighed through her tears, 'you're so good to me. I wish—I truly wish things could have been different.'

'Promise,' he persisted, and she nodded and tried a watery smile.

'I promise.'

They sat for a little longer, talking a little but staying for the most part silent. And when they got up at last to go back to Augusta, Flair was aware that their relationship had changed. There was a deeper companionship between them now; an understanding that hadn't been there before. Whatever happened, she knew that she and Lance would always be friends of a very special kind, and the knowledge warmed her lonely heart.

If only, she thought sadly as they got back into Lance's battered station wagon, she could have had even this much rapport with Luke.

By the time she woke next morning, Flair knew that the moment had come for her to leave Dougie and Lance. They had been good to her, they had given her the breathing space she needed; but now there was nothing more to be gained by staying. And it would be better for Lance, too, if she went, so that he could forget her, so that he could begin to live again as contentedly as he had before she arrived. His love hadn't gone deeply enough yet for him to be badly hurt, she was sure of that—but if she were to stay he could only be made more unhappy.

For his sake and for her own, she must leave.

Quietly she slipped out of bed and padded over to the window. It was a cool, slightly misty morning, and there was a little cloud on the horizon. It was still early enough for the weather to be uncertain, though when it did rain it never lasted for long, however heavily it might pour down. She re-

membered that day in the tingle forest with Luke
and the old familiar heat of longing washed over her
body. She hadn't heard of Luke since she left Perth,
and she wondered what he was doing. Probably
arranging his wedding with Roxanne, she thought
ruefully. Or maybe even married.

There had been a letter from Jeff waiting for her
when she arrived home with Lance last night. It had
told her little, beyond assuring her that everything
was all right and that he was keeping fit and busy—
all too busy, she thought bitterly, looking for work
to replace the contracts Luke had broken. He hadn't
mentioned Luke, but had said that he looked forward to seeing her soon. There was a wistful note
about the letter that caught at her heart. Perhaps
she ought to return to Perth. Her father was missing
her, it was plain. But until she felt more able to cope
with knowing that Luke was near, that she might
meet him at any time, she knew she couldn't do that.

The most sensible thing would be to look for another job, something that would occupy her too
active mind and take her through the days without
giving her time to brood. Turning away from the
window, she picked up a weekly paper and flicked it
open at the situations vacant columns. Maybe
there'd be something here.

She was never quite sure afterwards what made
her apply for the job in Geraldton. On paper, it
looked no better than any other job; yet as she read
it, she was seized with the determination to get it,
even if she had to drive up there and twist the
manager's arm to make him give it to her. She didn't
stop to wonder why.

Perhaps, she thought afterwards, it was because it was in the opposite direction from anywhere she had been with Luke. Just over three hundred miles north of Perth, it would be completely different. Somewhere that held no memories for her, somewhere she could start completely fresh. And as she went to the phone in the motel office and dialled the number given in the advertisement, her fingers shook with an excitement she hadn't felt for weeks. Perhaps there she could begin to forget Luke and live again.

She had begun to speak to the manager and was delighted to find that the vacancy hadn't been filled, when a sound made her look up. She saw the big station wagon roll into view outside, and her heart froze. Her voice died in her throat and it was only after her wildly jumping heart had steadied a little that she was aware of the man at the other end of the line asking if she was still there.

'Yes. . . .' she said vaguely, her eyes fixed on the tall figure getting out of the car, catching her breath at the way the sun shone on his burnished hair. 'Yes, I'm still here. . . . I'm sorry, I didn't catch what you said.'

'I asked if you could come up some time this week,' the voice repeated. 'Give it a go. No use talking about interviews when you're so far away, and you sound like the right person for us. What d'you say?'

Flair watched like a rabbit transfixed by a stoat as Luke swung easily across the paving towards the office. Her heart seemed to fill her throat. Why had he come? Was he looking for her? Panic-stricken, she tried to put an end to the conversation.

'Yes—yes, that'll be fine,' she heard herself say. 'I'll come right away. It shouldn't take more than a couple of days, should it? I can stop over in Perth tonight and come on up tomorrow. Yes, I'll be prepared to stay, a month at least. Yes, all right. I'll see you then.'

The office door was thrust open as she put down the phone. She stood rigid behind the desk as Luke shouldered his way in. Her knuckles whitened as she clutched the back of the chair, and she felt suddenly sick with apprehension.

Luke looked bigger than ever. He filled the doorway, seeming almost to swell as he saw her. His eyes, as bright and hard as diamonds, bored into her. His face was like granite.

'And just what was all that about?' he demanded. 'You've done it, have you? Broken young Lance's heart—and now you're looking for some new conquest. Well? Am I right?'

Flair's legs shook and she sat down suddenly at the desk. She ought to have remembered the flimsy walls of the office that allowed everything to be heard clearly from just outside. She stared up at Luke, remembering the last time she had seen him, the way he had left her almost naked and crying on his bed. A flush rose into her face at the memory, and she turned away sharply, but he was beside her at once, his fingers turning her chin none too gently, so that she had to look into his eyes.

'I reckoned you might have come to your senses by now,' he growled. 'Thought maybe we could talk. How about it, Flair?'

'There's nothing to talk about,' she managed, biting her lip.

'Nothing? That's not the way I see it. The way it strikes me, we've got one hell of a lot to talk about, and we might as well do it now as any other time.' He glanced around the shabby little office. 'But not here. Come on—we're going for a walk on the beach. It'll be pretty quiet this time of day.'

His fingers gripping her arm cruelly, he dragged Flair out of the office. She realised that he would drag her all the way if necessary and, once outside, stopped struggling and walked beside him as if she were willing. His fingers loosened a little but remained where they were; he wasn't going to risk her escaping, she realised as he led her along the beach.

'Now,' he said at last, stopping where a group of jagged rocks shielded them from the buildings. 'Now we can talk.'

'I told you,' Flair said shakily, 'there's nothing to talk about.'

'And I say there is!' His mouth was grim and hard. He obviously hadn't come to repeat his proposal. Not that she had ever thought he had—with a clear field for nearly three weeks, Roxanne would have made very sure by now that Luke was well and truly hers. Flair blinked back sudden tears and turned her head to look out at the restless sea.

'It's about your father, Flair,' Luke said then, surprising her. She looked at him, a tiny frown crinkling her brow.

'Dad? What about him?'

'What about him? What about *thinking* about

him?' Luke exclaimed in exasperation. 'Have you given him one single thought since you came down here to play fast and loose with young Lance——'

'I *didn't*!'

'——have you bothered that empty little head of yours for one moment, have you——'

'Now look here!' Flair blazed. 'Just who are you anyway to talk about my father like that? He's *my* father, not yours! He knows just why I'm here and he approves, so what's it got to do with you anyway? You don't own me or him, much as you may think you do. Why, you don't even employ me any more—or him, come to that—so what business is it of yours? *You* broke his contract—don't tell me you lie awake at nights worrying about him.'

Luke's fingers closed round her upper arms, digging into the soft flesh so that she almost cried out. His eyes glowed with anger as he brought his face close to hers and the furious colour mounted in his cheeks. Flair caught her breath as he pulled her close and she felt the hardness of his chest against her soft breasts. She squirmed against him, trying to escape, but felt excitement rising in spite of herself at the contact. Luke's hand left her arm, moving possessively across her back and down to press closely against the curves of her flank, and Flair felt her head begin to swim. From Luke's quickened breathing, she could tell that the pressure of their bodies against each other was affecting him too. She closed her eyes, felt her lips part and waited for his kiss, willing it to come; let her free hand creep up to his neck, twining her fingers in the hair that curled at the nape. She felt Luke's hands moving rhythmically up and down her thighs, stroking the bare skin under her short skirt and she clung to him, moving herself sensuously against him, longing for the fulfilment she had yearned for ever since their first meeting.

With a sudden groan that seemed to be torn from his very soul, Luke broke away, leaving her stunned and disbelieving. She looked up through tear-dewed lashes, and he took her firmly by the arm and sat her down on a smooth rock.

'We can't let this happen, Flair,' he told her roughly, his voice harsh with thwarted desire. 'Not with things as they are. . . . Look, I came to sort out this business about your father. Whatever else happens between us, I can't have you thinking the way you do about that. Just what did Jeff tell you about the contract?'

'That it had been broken,' she answered, bewildered by his insistence. 'Why? Have you changed your mind? Oh, Luke——'

'No, I haven't,' he cut in. 'The contracts are still off. But you've got it wrong——'

'Oh yes? Just what is there to get wrong? It all seems perfectly simple to me.' Flair scrambled to her feet and stood glaring down at him. 'And don't pretend you came all this way just to sort things out with me! You're too much the big tycoon to waste time on things like that!'

'I'm on my way to Albany, yes,' Luke admitted, but she let him go no further.

'Well, since you want it straight, here it is! Dad told me exactly what had happened about the contracts—I asked him and he told me it was true. There's nothing more to talk about as far as that's concerned. Not until you change your mind, anyway. And until then, I don't want to see you or speak to you again. I don't know why you even bothered to come here.' As she spoke, she backed away out of his reach, but Luke didn't seem to want to touch her now. For a moment she stared down at him, taking in the details of his appearance, the strength implicit in the lines of his body as he sat against the boulders, looking almost as if he were made of the same intractable stuff as the rock itself. Desire swept over her again and she turned angrily away, furious that even now she could still want him. 'Why can't you just go away and leave me alone?' she asked dully.

Luke stood up, uncoiling himself with the grace of a panther. He looked gravely down at her and said: 'You mean that, Flair? You know about your father and why the contracts were cancelled?'

'Oh, for goodness' sake why keep on about it?' she raged, wanted him to have done with talking, to take her in his arms again and this time finish what he'd so often started, even if it were for the only time in their lives. . . . 'Yes, I know, yes, yes, yes! What more do you want? What does it matter to you anyway?' She pushed her hair out of her eyes and stared up at him.

Luke watched her intently for a moment, his eyes questioning, unbelieving. Then a strange look, almost of disgust, distorted his rugged features and twisted the finely-chiselled lips. Bewildered and afraid, Flair backed away. She saw contempt dawn in his eyes, darkening them to a cold grey; saw scorn flick across his mouth as he spoke at last.

'Then I was right. You really are a cold-hearted little bitch. I told myself I was wrong—told myself I'd give you one more chance, come down here on my way to Albany and have one last talk with you. But you're not interested, are you, Flair? You don't really care about your father at all. You don't even think about him eating his heart out for you up there in Perth, wondering if——'

'Dad and I understand each other,' Flair interrupted, white with fury. 'He knew I had to get away. He knows I'm around if he needs me—but he doesn't, not really. Not after all these years. He's got used to being on his own.'

'Oh, there's no point talking to you,' Luke exclaimed contemptuously. 'You're interested in nothing but your own rotten skin. And your precious career, of course. Nobody else really means a thing to you, do they?' He looked her up and down and Flair flinched at the disgust in his eyes. 'You're even scared to get too involved in sex, much as your body wants it, because it just might get you in deeper than you can handle. Well, you do exactly what you've planned, Flair Pattison. Get on with your career. Don't let another person stand in your way. Because maybe you're right—maybe it is the only way you'll make a success of life. I know one thing—you're hell on wheels to anyone who happens to be unlucky enough to love you. I just hope that you'll see there aren't any more!'

Flair watched, too stricken to speak, as he turned aside and climbed over the rocks. He strode away along the beach and she knew that this was the last time; that he was striding out of her life for ever. Up till now, she realised, she had always had some hope that things would miraculously straighten themselves out, that somehow she and Luke would be able to meet without strain, without differences, and come together in harmony and love. But now that hope was gone. It faded and died like a starved plant as Luke walked along the beach, without looking back, and disappeared.

He had gone by the time Flair returned to the motel, and she was thankful. Lance and Dougie didn't mention him, though she knew they must have a good idea as to what had happened. Quietly, as if there were nothing else that mattered to her, Flair told them about the job in Geraldton, and they listened and nodded.

'Might be the best thing for you,' said Dougie, his bright gnome's eyes fixed on her face. 'Get a completely different scene, different people, you'd be surprised at the difference it makes. Sorry you couldn't stop around here, though.'

Flair avoided Lance's eyes. The way she felt now, she could easily break down and promise to stay, to marry him, to spend her life here. And it wouldn't work, she knew that. She had to resist the impulse to take the comfort she knew Lance could offer. She turned away.

'I'm sorry, too, Dougie. But there it is. You'll soon settle back and forget I was ever here.'

'I won't forget,' said Lance when she was ready to go. 'I won't ever forget, Flair. And what I said before still holds—if you ever need a friend. . . .'

'Oh, Lance!' Flair felt her eyes fill with tears. Why couldn't Luke be like this, affectionate, undemanding, loving? But if he was, she thought wryly, he wouldn't be Luke. And she probably wouldn't be in love with him. . . .

'It's best this way,' she said, and reached up to give Lance a kiss. 'I know it wouldn't work out between us—but I'll always want you as a friend, Lance, if you'll have me.'

He lifted her case into the car and slammed the hatchback door. 'Well, you know where I am, then.' He came round and touched her cheek gently. 'Take care of yourself, Flair. And get things sorted out with Luke, if you can. He's a fine man. If I have to lose you, I couldn't lose you to a better guy.'

Chance would be a fine thing, Flair thought, but she didn't say so. Time would show Lance that there was no way she and Luke would be getting together again. She climbed into the driving seat and leaned out to give Dougie a farewell kiss as he came out into the bright sunshine.

And then the motel was behind her. Yet another stage of her life in Australia was over. She turned on to the now familiar highway and headed for Perth, for an overnight stop with her father before going on to begin the next, in the northerly town of Geraldton.

But Jeff wasn't there when she arrived at the house in Yokine. Surprised, a little uneasy, she paced through the rooms. They were all as usual; a little tidier than she remembered, perhaps, but Jeff wasn't an untidy man anyway. The house seemed empty, and she chided herself for having fancies. Just because he wasn't home didn't mean there was anything wrong, did it? Couldn't a man go out for the evening occasionally? But there was something that told her this was more than an evening out. Well then, couldn't he stay away for a day or two? Maybe there was a woman in his life, someone he hadn't told Flair about. Was there any reason why there shouldn't be? Any reason why a man like Jeff, not yet old, still attractive, shouldn't find love?

Scolding herself for her irrational fears, Flair made herself an omelette and some coffee and went to bed. She had an early start tomorrow and if Jeff didn't come home soon she'd have to leave without seeing him. She hoped it wouldn't be that way; but though she lay awake for a while, she was too exhausted, both from emotion and from her long day, to fight sleep for long, and soon her eyes closed and she slipped effortlessly into dreams.

It was early when she woke, disappointed to find that her father was still not home. She stifled thoughts of accidents and, telling herself again that he must be staying with friends, showered, dressed and made toast before taking some orange juice from the fridge and wandering out into the sunlit garden to eat her breakfast. Perhaps Jeff would arrive before she had to leave.

But once in the garden, by the pool, her thoughts returned inevitably to Luke. Their first meeting had been here, she recalled, glancing at the still blue water where she had been floating when he had first appeared. Even then she had been aware of his almost animal magnetism, the sheer blatant maleness that surrounded him like an aura. She remembered the way he had stood there, casual yet alert like a

great cat, the way he had moved with the suddenness
and grace of a panther when he had lifted her from
the water; the strength and power she had sensed in
his body as he held her close.

Waves of desire flowed over her even now as she
recalled those moments. And there had been others
too; that morning on Blue Island, when she had
woken to find herself in his bed. The day he had
caught her in the streaming rain under the tingle
trees and told her that he loved her and wanted to
marry her . . . the angry scene in his bedroom at the
hotel, when he had stripped her, rousing her senses
to such a pitch that she could only beg for his love;
the delicious contact on the beach at Augusta, just
before he walked for ever out of her life. . . .

She lay back in the lounger, feeling the sun hot on
her closed eyelids as tears squeezed between them
and trickled slowly down her cheeks. It would have
been better if she had never met Luke Seager, she
thought unhappily. Nothing but heartache and
sorrow had come of it. He had revealed to her a
desire and love that she had never suspected. She
would have been better off never knowing about it,
better off remaining singleminded, thinking only of
her career, following the path her mother had
mapped out for her. Susan was right, she told herself
sadly. Love got in the way of living. It distracted
you and even if it made you happy for a while—and
some of those moments with Luke would remain for
ever cherished in her heart—it left you cold and
lonely in the end.

With a sudden decisive movement, Flair swung
herself from the lounger and went back into the

house. From now on, she would start life anew. She would stop thinking of Luke Seager, stop hoping that somehow things would come right for them, stop yearning for his kisses. From now on, she would put him out of her mind as he had walked out of her life. She would take up her own life again, where she had left off when he had appeared in her heart. From this moment, she was once again Flair Pattison, career girl.

Leaving a note for her father to tell him where she was going, Flair set off for her new destination. Geraldton was over three hundred miles north of Perth, approaching the tropics, but the highway, leading directly there from the city, was straight and virtually empty. She drove steadily, meeting only the occasional truck or station wagon, and as she drove the beauty of the bush began once again to soak into her and calm her fevered thoughts. How could anyone describe Australia as barren? she wondered as she drove past stretches of plain carpeted brilliantly with the crimson colours of desert peas, scarlet banksia and red-flowered gums, the glowing golds of native buttercups, black kangaroo paw and bull banksia, and the speedwell blue of leschenaultia, all tumbled together in glorious confusion. At other points the taller species fringed the road; slender eucalyptus with their grey trunks and silvery-green leaves, wattles and the strange little 'black boys'— stumpy trunks with a mop of fibrous, grass-like 'hair' on top, which Flair had been told took centuries to grow and were as hard as iron.

Now and then she passed farms, their buildings set well back from the road, often with a dam nearby

filled with cool water collected during the winter.
Once or twice she came upon a settlement, consisting
usually of a fuel station and a restaurant and little
else. She was glad to stop and fill her tanks, taking
the opportunity for a long cool drink in the air-con-
ditioned café as well. The air was growing noticeably
hotter as she drove north, and the sun beat down
more strongly than she had yet experienced, particularly when she was in the cooler region south of
Perth.

It was late afternoon before she finally arrived in
Geraldton. Thankfully, she drove down the wide
main street, taking pleasure in the well laid out little
port and the signs of prosperity that showed in attrac-
tively-designed houses and neat hotels. She had
noticed too the productive farming area that lay
around the town, and she saw with delight the fishing
boats and the Abrolhos Islands that lay offshore like
jewels in the sparkling sea.

Yes, she decided as she drew up at last outside the
hotel, this was the place where she could start her
life anew. This was the place where she could find
happiness at last.

She stepped out of the car, conscious of the stiffness
that comes with a long drive. A tiny flutter of nervousness stirred in her stomach, as she wondered
what her new employer would be like. Not another
Luke Seager, she hoped! She didn't think she could
cope with that.

The hotel entrance was pleasantly cool, air-condi-
tioned, with huge pot-plants giving it a welcoming
appearance. It was attractively furnished, though
completely unpretentious, and Flair felt her interest

quicken as she stepped through the fly-screens and caught the eye of the pretty, dark-haired receptionist behind the desk. In another moment the manager was with her and she smiled at him, liking at once his pleasant craggy face.

Then her brows contracted as she noticed the almost embarrassed expression in his eyes. He returned her smile vaguely, as if his thoughts were elsewhere, and shook his head when Flair mentioned bringing in her luggage.

'Look, Miss Pattison,' he said at last, his embarrassment acutely obvious by now, 'I think it'd be better if you went straight to your room. There's someone come to see you—it looks as if you might have to change your plans.'

'Change my plans?' Flair stared at him. 'I don't know what you're talking about. I've been looking forward to working here and I like Geraldton already. Anyway, I don't know anyone here—there must be some mistake.'

The manager's face turned red and he rubbed the back of his neck awkwardly. 'No, there's no mistake. Look, I'm as sorry about it as you are, and if you want to come back here any time—well, in the next couple of weeks anyway—I'll keep the job open for you, can't say fairer than that. But you'd better go and see your visitor. He'll explain it all to you.'

Bewildered, Flair followed him through airy corridors to her room. She could not understand what had happened, and inside she was crying out in protest at this further interference in her life. Just as she was hoping to get settled at last—who could this possibly be, waiting for her the moment she arrived, proclaiming a change in plans that she knew nothing of?

Various thoughts flew through her mind, but she could come to no conclusion. Her appointment here had happened so suddenly that she could not believe that anyone she knew could have arrived in Geraldton before her. And anyway, why should they? Why should anyone want to prevent her taking up this new job?

The manager opened the door and Flair stepped into a spacious room, shaded from the sun by venetian blinds, as pleasantly furnished as the rest of the hotel—a room she could be happy in. Her resentment grew at the unwarranted interference in her plans. She turned, looking for her unknown visitor— and gasped with pure amazement.

'You!' she whispered as Luke uncoiled himself from a large basket chair and stood tall and uncompromising in the centre of the room. 'I might have known it! But—how? Why? What do you want of me now? Can't you leave me alone? *Do you have to persecute me like this?*'

CHAPTER TEN

LUKE moved slightly so that she could see his face more clearly, and she was shaken by the grimness of his hard mouth. He crossed over and looked down at her, his gaze penetrating, with a shadow of scorn somewhere behind it and she met it with a puzzled frown shading her own sea-green eyes.

'I'm not persecuting you,' he said harshly. 'Believe me, if there'd been anyone else to send I'd have sent them. Do you think I *want* to spend my life chasing you about all over W.A.? Do you think I'd have come at all if it hadn't been important? You've got to come back to Perth, Flair, and you've got to come now.'

'Oh, I have, have I?' Flair was just about at the end of her tether. She had been looking forward, after her long drive, to settling in to her new home, getting to know new people and tackling a new job. She had intended pushing Luke Seager right out of her mind, back to the limbo he had been in before she knew him. And now this! 'Didn't I make it clear to you that you don't have the running of my life? When are you going to learn that I don't come running just because you happen to crook your little finger. . . .'

'And when are *you* going to learn that I don't play games?' he cut in furiously. 'Yes, Flair, you *do* come when I call, because I don't call for nothing, do you

understand that? My God, ever since you set foot in
this country you've thought *you* could call the tune,
you've thought it was all set up just for you, just for
one spoilt little English girl—it never occurred to
you that anyone else might matter, did it? Never
struck you *we've* got lives to live too, lives that were
doing very nicely, thank you, until you happened
along.' His hand shot up and tangled in her hair.
Flair jerked away involuntarily and gasped with
pain as the hair pulled agonisingly at her scalp.
Goaded almost beyond endurance, she glared at
Luke and raised her hands, fingers crooked, to claw
at his face. But before she could touch him he had
both her slender wrists in one huge fist and had
pulled her close, too close even to kick at his shins as
she longed to do.

'Just be still and listen for a few minutes, will you,'
he grated, and she felt his breath fan her cheek. 'You
seem to have a very exalted idea of your importance,
don't you? Do you really think I've come all this
way just for the ride? Do you really think it's just
because I'm yearning for a sight of your pretty little
face? I've got business to attend to, you know. I'm
not out on a picnic.'

'So why don't you tell me what it is?' she flashed.
'This important business that's brought you up
here—why don't you tell me, and then you can get
out and go back where you came from? Because I'm
not going back, you know—whatever it is that's so
important it's brought you up here to wreck my life
yet again, I'm *not* giving it up, I'm *not* going back!
So the quicker we get this over and you go, the better
it'll be for both of us.'

His compelling eyes were like gimlets as they searched her face. 'Just as I thought,' he growled at last. 'That's why I didn't ring, didn't leave a message. I tried to tell myself that you weren't that callous— that you'd drop everything and come. But I knew you wouldn't. I knew you'd just shrug it aside, just like you did before. I knew I'd have to drag you every inch of the way.'

'I don't know what you're talking about,' Flair said wearily. 'Shrug it aside—callous—what on earth is it all about?'

The scorn was naked now in his eyes, deepening to utter contempt as his lip curled, and Flair flinched away from the expression that wounded her, even as she told herself it didn't matter.

'Your father's what I'm talking about,' he told her curtly. 'Remember him—the fellow you came out to see? The fellow who's had to worry and wonder about you, who didn't even know where you were last night? Or maybe you've forgotten him already. Now you've got your nice little career on the go again, I suppose he doesn't matter any——'

'Stop it!' she screamed. 'Stop! What *about* Dad?' A flicker of fear ran chillingly up her spine and she shook her trapped arms helplessly. 'What's happened? For heaven's sake, what's happened?'

'Did you go home last night?' Luke asked, and she nodded impatiently.

'Yes. Dad wasn't there, so I left him a note.' Her eyes widened as she realised what she'd said. 'That's how you knew just where I was heading, isn't it? You've seen the note. *But what about Dad?*'

'Jeff was already in hospital when you arrived,'

Luke told her flatly. 'He'd gone in for some tests. In the early hours of this morning he had an attack—they tried to get you, but no one knew where you were or how to get hold of you. Jeff wasn't in any state to tell them himself, even if he'd known, and nobody thought you might actually be at home. Eventually they got on to me. I went in to see him and decided you'd better be found, and quick. I went to the house to see if you'd written, or phoned a message through—he'd left the answerphone set. I found your note.'

Flair's face was chalk white, her eyes two huge green pools. She tried to speak, but her voice wouldn't work. She cleared her throat and tried again, and this time managed a thin, dry whisper.

'Dad—*ill?* An attack—what sort of attack? Why wasn't I told he was going into hospital? How—how bad is he?'

'What do you think?' he answered brutally. 'Look, Flair, I'm not wrapping it up for you. You must have known this was on the cards. Yes, Jeff's in a pretty poor way, though they're doing all they can for him, and it's not helping that he doesn't know where you are from one day to the next. You've been nothing but a damned worry to him from the moment you arrived, don't you realise that? Or do you think he just sits back and smiles and thinks you're amusing? You know, you make me sick! "*What sort of attack?*"' he mimicked cruelly. 'A *heart* attack, of course, what else? And as for you not being told he was going in to hospital—are you really trying to tell me that would have made one scrap of difference to your precious plans? And that Jeff wasn't well aware of that?'

'Dad . . .!' Flair whispered, staring sightlessly at the bands of evening sunlight that sloped through the venetian blinds across the cool tiled floor. 'Dad . . . I've got to get to him. . . .'

'That was the general idea,' Luke agreed sarcastically. 'That was why I came up. To get you back as fast as possible. And not for your sake, either,' he shot at her. 'For Jeff's—though I don't know why it should matter to him!'

Flair turned her dazed eyes on him. He had released her arms now and she stood rubbing them absently, unaware of the fact that there would be a faint ring of bruises round each wrist. Her mind, shocked into numbness by the news and Luke's brutal way of breaking it to her, had begun to function again, and she stared at him wonderingly.

'How *did* you get up here so quickly?' she asked. 'If you didn't leave until after I did—and you didn't pass me anywhere on the road, I'm sure, unless it was when I was filling the tank somewhere—how did you get here before me?'

'The same way we're going back,' Luke said tersely. 'I flew. And that's why we need to be on our way as soon as possible—it'll be dark before long, and although it's not a long flight I'd sooner make it in daylight if I can. So can we go now?' His voice was sardonic. 'You needn't worry about your car—I brought a man up with me, he'll drive it back tomorrow.'

'My—car?' Still shaken, Flair passed a hand across her forehead. Then her eyes widened. 'You *flew*? But is there a plane back? I——'

'I flew *myself*,' he told her in tones of extreme patience, as if talking to a child. 'Look, let's cut the chatter, Flair, and get on our way. I've explained everything to your friend here, he understands the position.' He took her arm, more gently this time, and his glance swept over her face. 'It's been a bit of a shock to you, this, hasn't it? Well, maybe you'll take a bit more notice of other people another time. Jeff's never been one to complain about nothing, but maybe you didn't know that.' And before she could ask what he meant, he was sweeping her out of the room. 'My driver's been having a meal. He'll drive us out to the airfield and then we can get moving.'

'I didn't even know you had an aeroplane,' Flair murmured as they arrived at the civil airfield and she saw the smart little Cessna parked near the perimeter. A feeling of nervousness shivered through her limbs as she looked at it. She had only ever flown in the jumbo jet that had brought her to Australia—and this looked tiny!

'There's a lot you don't know about me,' Luke said shortly. He nodded to the mechanic who came up to them. 'Everything okay, Pete? Right—we'll be away, then. Get in, Flair.'

It was obvious that he was going to make no concessions at all to her lack of experience and any possible nerves. Silently, Flair climbed aboard and sat down where he showed her, strapping herself in securely. The engine roared into life and the tiny aircraft began to move. She closed her eyes. Now, more than at any time, she longed desperately for the comfort of Luke's strong arms, even the reassurance of a glance from those compelling blue eyes.

But for all Luke was concerned, she might not have been there. And her thoughts were sad and bitter as they flew south down the coast and back into Perth.

At any other time, Flair would have thrilled to the pleasure and beauty of that flight. The sweeping coastline below, the intense blue of the sea laced with white surf; the colours of the bush, painted with the red glow of the setting sun; finally the tower blocks of Perth beside the broad curving slash of the Swan river—all these made a picture that imprinted itself for ever in her mind, yet which she could not enjoy. Her thoughts were too taken up with anxiety over her father, and unhappiness at Luke's intractable and hostile attitude.

And if he thought it was her fault, she thought with sudden anger, how much blame should be laid at his door? The merger—the broken contract— hadn't those things worried Jeff just as much? Weren't they as likely to have caused the stress and uncertainty that had brought on this devastating attack?

Perhaps that had never occurred to Luke. But when all this was over, Flair was going to make sure he knew that it had occured to her. On that, she was determined.

At last they were back in Perth, touching down softly, to be met by another of Luke's drivers with the big Holden. Agonising pictures filled Flair's mind as they drove back through the darkened streets of the city. No wonder Dad had been looking tired lately! She had noticed it so many times—at that first moment of meeting at the airport, even.

She cursed herself for not having realised there was something seriously wrong, for having accepted his explanation about a heavy workload, for not having insisted that he see a doctor or at least take things easier.

And Luke—she could kill him, she thought viciously, she could strangle him with her bare hands. He *must* have seen the difference in her father. Yet he had continued to demand more and more work from him—the island complex, the Albany motel, all the smaller alterations he was making to other properties that nevertheless piled up into a lot of work and worry. And then, having created as much stress as he could, he took the whole lot away at a moment's notice. Took away her father's livelihood, in effect, for surely by then Seager Hotels must have formed the bulk of Jeff's work. No wonder her father had grown older and greyer, no wonder he was now lying in hospital recovering from a heart attack. And at that thought her own heart contracted with fear— suppose he *wasn't* recovering. . . .

And now they were in the forecourt of the hospital and the driver had stopped to let them out. Her heart hammering, Flair got out and joined Luke, following him through the main door. Neither of them spoke. Luke's face was grim, and Flair was too sick with fear to say a word.

The corridors seemed to go on for ever, but Luke clearly knew his way about them and strode along without glancing at Flair, who had almost to run to keep up with him. By now, fear was pricking her skin all over. Suppose Jeff was worse? Suppose—but she pushed the thought away hastily. He *had* to be still alive. The idea haunted her that while she'd been sleeping comfortably at home, he'd been in here, fighting for his life. If only she'd known! If only she'd tried to find out where he was.

She glanced at Luke, striding ahead. If things had been different, he would have been her support and comfort now. She felt suddenly bereft, realising that she couldn't turn to him for help and knowing with a sudden despairing clarity that he was the one man on earth who *could* help. If only everything hadn't gone wrong, she thought hopelessly, she and Luke would have belonged to each other. But there were too many barriers between them. Roxanne—the merger—the broken contract—there was no way she could go to him for comfort, no way he would give it. Because he too had shown an inexplicable hostility. Something else that she still didn't understand came between them when he looked at her, something that brought scorn and contempt into his eyes.

They were at the door to the ward, and Luke paused to speak to the duty nurse, while Flair stood by feeling sick with dread. She closed her eyes with relief when she heard the nurse say that Jeff was still alive and holding his own; and then she felt Luke's hand under her arm and raised her face to look up at him.

Even now, his expression was remote and shuttered, and Flair felt the hot tears in her eyes. Couldn't he see that she needed the comfort only he could give? Couldn't he, even now, drop those barriers and help her? But the hostility in his glance told her the answer. He couldn't. Wouldn't. There was nothing between them now but dislike.

Jeff was their only link.

'You'd better go in on your own,' said Luke. 'They don't want him to have too much excitement. He may be asleep, of course.'

Trembling, Flair tiptoed into the ward. It was very small; there were two other beds, but she hardly noticed them. Her eyes were for Jeff, lying as white as the sheets that covered him. Jeff, whose eyes, more grey than green now, opened slowly as she approached; who smiled faintly but with all the old affection and lifted a pale hand weakly from the bed in greeting.

'Oh, Dad,' said Flair, and felt her eyes fill with tears.

She mustn't cry though, mustn't upset him. Gently, she kissed him and sat down beside the bed, stroking his hand.

'Luke brought me,' she told him as his eyes watched her face. 'Do you know, I was at home last night—if only I'd known you were here! Why didn't you tell me you were coming in for tests, Dad? I'd have come straight back.'

'I didn't want you worried.' The tired eyes searched hers. 'You haven't been happy, Flair. I made Luke promise . . .!'

Flair frowned. 'Made him promise what? Dad, Luke hasn't told me anything. What was it he promised?'

'Made him promise not to tell you I was ill.' The voice was weaker now. 'I wanted to see you settle down happily. . . . He's a fine man, Flair. That contract—he only cancelled it because I had to back out. The doctors said . . . he gave me good terms,

Flair. . . . Wish you and he could get things straight. . . .'

Flair stared at him. His words didn't make sense. She wanted to ask more questions, get the full story, but she knew she mustn't worry him now.

'Fine man . . .! Jeff was muttering. 'Been a son to me, Flair . . . and now I've got my daughter too. . . .'

'Dad,' she whispered. 'Dad, don't think about it. Don't worry. Everything's going to be all right, Dad, all you've got to do is get better. It's all right— everything's all right.'

She was aware of Luke coming quietly to her side and she looked up at him, all the barriers down, all her love and fear showing at last in her face. Her heart sang at the implication behind Jeff's words, and she searched Luke's face for the truth. For a moment, their eyes held, acknowledging that now, for the time being at least, their own feelings must be put aside for Jeff's sake, that somehow he must be given hope, something to live for. . . . Then Luke bent down too and said softly:

'Jeff? Can you hear me? We've got some news for you, Flair and I. We were going to tell you later— but we can't keep it secret any longer.' He paused and Flair caught her breath. 'We're engaged! I want to marry your daughter, Mr Pattison.' He fished in his pocket and drew out a small box, and Flair watched, fascinated, unable to believe what was happening. 'Here's the ring,' said Luke, and with Jeff's tired eyes on them he picked up Flair's hand and slid the ring on to her engagement finger. Then he kissed her, gently, on the lips and once again she felt the tears on her lashes.

'Do I have your consent?' Luke asked quietly, and Flair saw her father smile faintly before he gave an almost imperceptible nod and whispered: 'Just so long as I can be there to give her away. . . .'

'That's a promise,' said Luke. 'But don't be too long about it, will you?'

Jeff's eyes closed and the nurse, who had been attending to one of the other beds, came over and gave him a quick, professional glance. 'You'll have to go now,' she murmured. 'Mr Pattison needs all his strength for getting better.' She regarded the figure in the bed and nodded. 'You've done him good, though. He looks more relaxed now. You can come back later, just for a short visit.'

Silent again, Flair and Luke walked back through the corridors to the entrance. Flair was dazed and bewildered. Too much had happened in those few minutes for her to take in. Back at the car, she stopped and looked up at Luke, trying to read the expression in his face. But Luke was inscrutable. He looked down at her and as she searched his eyes all she could decide was that the hostility had disappeared, at least for the time being.

'Luke?' she said timidly, and felt a flicker of nerves as he put up a finger and touched her cheek.

'I think we've got some more talking to do, don't you, Flair?' he said quietly. 'Get things sorted out once and for all. Will you come back to the hotel?' He opened the door. 'We'll come back and see him again later.'

Flair got in beside him. His face was still unreadable, and she wondered what he intended to say. That the engagement was off, of course; it had never been real, just something to give her father hope, to bring him back to life. Later on it could be broken again, and this time for good.

She looked down at the opal, her eyes misted with tears. The red and blue colours glowed up at her and she wondered why Luke had had it in his pocket; maybe he'd intended this, knowing that it could help her father. But it didn't help her—it just twisted the knife in the wound.

Luke said nothing until they were in his suite at the top of the hotel. Flair sat down in one of the comfortable chairs, looking round the familiar room. The last time she had been here had been that day when Luke had thrown her on to his bed like a rag doll, and later left her crying and lost. She had never thought to come back again. But although she was back, she knew that what had happened then could never happen again. Two days ago, on the beach at Augusta, Luke had walked away from her for the last time. Nothing could change that.

Luke stood by the window, staring out, and she knew that the silence had to come to an end. He had said they had to talk—well, she would start it off.

'You'll be wanting your ring back,' she said, watching his stiff back. 'Don't worry, Luke—I won't hold you to it. I know you only did it for Dad's sake.'

He whipped round. 'What are you talking about?'

'The ring—the engagement. I realise you didn't mean it. I won't make a scene, you don't have to worry.' She stared at him, frightened suddenly by the dawning emotion in his eyes. 'Luke, what is it?'

Terrified, she began to struggle with the ring, pulling it from her finger, but before she could do so he was at her side, his hands holding hers, keeping them apart, pushing the ring back violently. *'Luke!'*

'Leave it there!' His face was a torment of conflicting emotions. 'Flair, I can't take much more of this. You're driving me crazy and you don't even know it. Have you any idea—any idea at all—what I've been going through since you came to Australia?'

Bewildered, still frightened, Flair shook her head. 'Luke, I——'

He laid his fingers against her lips. 'Don't say anything. I know this isn't the best time to say this, but if I don't get things sorted out I'm going to go mad. Flair, tell me the truth. Did you or did you not know why that contract was cancelled?'

Flair shook her bronze head helplessly. 'I—I don't know. I thought I did. I thought it was because of the merger, because Hailey Ryan wanted his own men used. That's what Roxanne told me—but just now, Dad said it was because he was ill. At least, I *thought* that was what he said. Did he *know* he was ill, Luke? Why didn't he tell me, if he did?'

Luke's eyes pierced hers, diamond hard.

'Is that the truth, Flair? You didn't know he was ill, had heart trouble? You didn't know his doctors had told him to think about retiring, or at least giving up all his work with me because it was too stressful? You honestly didn't know that?'

'No—I didn't know anything. I had no idea.'

'Then why the merry hell did you pretend you did?' he exploded, so suddenly that Flair gasped and drew back.

'What do you mean? I never pretended I knew anything?'

'You did—when I asked you if Jeff had told you everything, you said yes. You said you knew all about the cancellation of the contract. Naturally, I thought that meant you knew he was ill—I thought you were a callous little bitch because you just didn't seem to care, you seemed concerned only about the money he wouldn't be earning any more. You went off and left him worried to death about you, and the fact that that wasn't helping his illness just didn't seem to get through to you at all. You——'

'But I didn't *know*!' Flair interrupted furiously. 'I didn't have any idea he was ill, not until today. Oh, I thought he looked tired, but whenever I mentioned it he laughed and fobbed me off. I told you I knew about the cancellation because I thought I did. I thought he *had* told me everything. How was I to know——' She broke off, staring at Luke with angry green eyes. 'But *you* knew! You knew all the time. Why didn't *you* tell me?'

'Because he made me promise not to.' Luke's voice was weary. 'He wanted you to settle down and be happy here, he didn't want you worried by anything. I told him you ought to know, but he wouldn't have it. He wanted you to be happy.'

'Oh God,' muttered Flair, burying her face in her hands. 'And I was too wrapped up in myself to notice. Why didn't I see?'

'Because he didn't want you to.' She felt Luke's hand touch her cheek, stroking the soft skin tenderly. 'Flair, look at me.' He raised her chin so that she had to meet his eyes and she gasped at the expression in them, their sudden tender darkening. 'Flair, we've got ourselves into one hell of a muddle over this, haven't we? And before we go back to that hospital this evening, we've got to get things straight.' He paused and drew her closer and she felt an overwhelming sense of homecoming as she came into his arms at last. 'Flair, you've got to trust me, now and always. No more running off because some spoiled little bitch spins you a yarn, get that? From now on, it's *me* you believe.'

Flair rubbed her cheek against his, delighting in the faint roughness of his skin. 'You mean Roxanne? But the merger——'

'That's her father's business, not hers. And whatever she may think, Hailey Ryan's too astute a man to wish on his daughter a marriage that can't work. Yes, she did make a play for me—but Hailey and I did some straight talking. I told him Roxanne would never make a partner for me, nor I for her, and he understood. He wants to see her happy—not tied to money. She doesn't need to marry a rich man, and he doesn't care who she chooses so long as there's love there.' Luke stopped and laid his lips against Flair's cheek. 'He's a sensible man, is Hailey Ryan.'

'So you're not marrying Roxanne. . . .' Flair breathed, thrilling at the touch of his hands as they moved caressingly over her body.

'No way!' He chuckled, then said on a groan, 'Oh, Flair, if you knew what I went through that day you ran out on me. It was a nightmare! I just couldn't believe it had really happened. Just when everything seemed so marvellous. I hated you, I hated Roxanne, I hated myself most of all.' He held her close, hard against him. 'Don't ever do that to me again, Flair.'

She pressed against him, tears spilling from her eyes as she thought of his pain. She had suffered too—but surely now they were truly together again, surely now nothing could part them. She raised her hand and looked over Luke's shoulder at the opal ring. The stone of Australia—the stone that bound her to Luke for ever.

'Luke,' she whispered as she found his lips with hers. 'Luke, I don't want to be parted from you ever again. I want you to love me—love me now, so that nothing can come between us.'

He drew away a little and looked into her eyes, his own so dark that they were almost black. 'You mean that?'

Flair nodded. As he ran his hands down her body she shivered, a violent, uncontrollable shudder of pure rapture. She raised her hands and let them wander down his chest, unbuttoning his shirt as they went; pulled the soft material aside and reached up to nuzzle her face in the soft hairs. Luke made an inarticulate sound and held her to him, his fingers fumbling with the fastening of her own clothes, and they lay close together, revelling in the touch of skin against skin, feeling the beating of each other's heart against their own, kissing, caressing, exploring. The friction had gone out of their relationship at last; there was nothing now that could come between them, raising the ugliness of mistrust or jealousy to spoil their love. And as Flair lay stretched beneath him, feeling the sinuous movements of his body against hers, experiencing at last the joy of complete fulfilment, she knew that here was her life and her love, a steady flame that would burn through the rest of their lives to comfort and strengthen them both.

At last, the surging of their blood quietened, they lay closely entwined in the contentment and happiness that followed the storm of desire. Their bodies moulded softly together, as if they had no bones. Slowly they returned to reality, and at last Flair, reminded now of the one remaining anxiety in her life, said:

'Luke. Will—will Dad really be all right?'

'Yes, he will,' Luke reassured her. 'He was in the right place when it happened—if he hadn't been, it might have been a different story. And now that he's seen you—he's really on the mend, Flair, I can promise you that.'

'He'll be happy when we get married,' she murmured drowsily. 'It will have to be soon, Luke—as soon as he's fit to give me away, as we promised.'

'And that could be sooner than you think, my darling,' he answered, letting his fingers tease her into a gasp of delight. 'We'll be married by his bedside—the moment he can sit up. Meanwhile. . . .' He pulled her close again and desire pulsed once more through her body, so that she whimpered and clung to him. 'It won't be long before we have to get ready to go and see him again,' he murmured into her throat. 'Any ideas how we can pass the time until then?'

And she knew that they were in perfect agreement at last.

Harlequin® |Plus|

THE RAUCOUS KOOKABURRA

Shortly after her arrival in Perth, Australia, Flair hears the ''raucous laughter'' of a kookaburra. This little bird is indigenous to Australia, and its peculiar name is appropriate. The kookaburra has a short squat grayish brown body, with a stubby little tail on one end and a rather large head on the other. But the strangest characteristic is its song—which can hardly be said to be musical. Instead it is a fiendish-sounding maniacal bray, easily distinguishable in the open woodlands the bird inhabits.

The kookaburra is a member of the kingfisher family, and although most people think kingfishers live near water, many species, including kookaburras, are forest dwellers. And while they prefer the countryside, they can also be seen in city parks and gardens and have been known to become friendly enough to accept food from a person's outstretched hand.

The laughter of the kookaburra is usually heard early in the morning and again each evening just after sunset. As a result, Australians have nicknamed it the ''bushman's clock.'' There is a story the native people of Australia tell about this bird: when the god Bayame created the sun and made it rise for the first time, he gave the kookaburra its strange, raucous, almost human laughter in order to wake up mankind so they could witness and admire the first dawn!

ANNE ❀ WEALE

FLORA

A new epic-length historical-romance bestseller!

It was the turn of the century…

Flora Jackson, an orphan of British and Chinese descent, had been raised in a mission in western China. Saved from slaughter by Englishman Caspar Lomax, she had no choice but to journey with him to Shanghai. After she was taken advantage of by the unscrupulous madam of a local bordello, Lomax offered Flora a marriage of convenience and safe passage to England. In England Flora discovered a new and disturbing life…and experienced a passion she'd never dreamed possible.

Available now wherever paperback books are sold, or send your name, address and zip or postal code, along with a check or money order for $4.70 (includes 75¢ for postage and handling), payable to Harlequin Reader Service, to:

Harlequin Reader Service

In the U.S.
P.O. Box 22188
Tempe, AZ 85282

In Canada
649 Ontario Street
Stratford, Ontario N5A 6W2

FLORA-2

Take these
4 best-selling
novels
FREE

as advertised on TV

Yes! Four sophisticated,
contemporary love stories
by four world-famous
authors of romance
FREE, as your
introduction to the Harlequin Presents
subscription plan. Thrill to **Anne Mather**'s
passionate story BORN OUT OF LOVE, set
in the Caribbean.... Travel to darkest Africa
in **Violet Winspear**'s TIME OF THE TEMPTRESS....Let
Charlotte Lamb take you to the fascinating world of London's
Fleet Street in MAN'S WORLD .... Discover beautiful Greece in
Sally Wentworth's moving romance SAY HELLO TO YESTERDAY.

Harlequin Presents...

*The very finest
in romance fiction*

Join the millions of avid Harlequin readers all over the
world who delight in the magic of a really exciting novel.
EIGHT great NEW titles published EACH MONTH!
Each month you will get to know exciting, interesting,
true-to-life people .... You'll be swept to distant lands you've
dreamed of visiting .... Intrigue, adventure, romance, and
the destiny of many lives will thrill you through each
Harlequin Presents novel.

Get all the latest books before they're sold out!
As a Harlequin subscriber you actually receive your
personal copies of the latest Presents novels immediately
after they come off the press, so you're sure of getting all
8 each month.

Cancel your subscription whenever you wish!
You don't have to buy any minimum number of books.
Whenever you decide to stop your subscription just let us
know and we'll cancel all further shipments.

Your **FREE** gift includes

Anne Mather—Born out of Love
Violet Winspear—Time of the Temptress
Charlotte Lamb—Man's World
Sally Wentworth—Say Hello to Yesterday

FREE Gift Certificate
and subscription reservation

Mail this coupon today!

Harlequin Reader Service

In the U.S.A.
1440 South Priest Drive
Tempe, AZ 85281

In Canada
649 Ontario Street
Stratford, Ontario N5A 6W2

Please send me my 4 Harlequin Presents books free. Also, reserve a subscription to the 8 new Harlequin Presents novels published each month. Each month I will receive 8 new Presents novels at the low price of $1.75 each [*Total—$14.00 a month*]. There are no shipping and handling or any other hidden charges. I am free to cancel at any time, but even if I do, these first 4 books are still mine to keep absolutely FREE without any obligation.   SB589

Offer expires October 31, 1983

NAME	(PLEASE PRINT)
ADDRESS	APT. NO.
CITY	
STATE/PROV.	ZIP/POSTAL CODE

If price changes are necessary you will be notified.